Homosexual Intifada

I0880590

HOMOSEXUAL INTIFADA

A QUEER PALESTINIAN ANTHOLOGY

Edited by **George Abraham** and **Hannah Moushabeck**

Interlink Books

An imprint of Interlink Publishing Group, Inc.
Northampton, Massachusetts

First published in 2026 by

Interlink Books
An imprint of Interlink Publishing Group, Inc.
46 Crosby Street
Northampton, Massachusetts 01060
www.interlinkbooks.com

Copyright © Interlink Publishing Group, Inc., 2026
All contributors retain copyright of their works.
Cover art by Bint Bandora

All rights reserved. No part of this publication may be reproduced, stored in a retrieval system or transmitted, in any form or by any means, without the prior written permission of the publisher. Without limiting the exclusive rights of any author, contributor, or the publisher of this publication, any unauthorized use of this publication to train generative artificial intelligence (AI) technologies is expressly prohibited.

Library of Congress Cataloging-in-Publication Data available
ISBN 978-1-62371-568-7

10 9 8 7 6 5 4 3 2

Printed and bound in the United States of America

For our Ghazzawi kin, surviving siege after impossible siege,
teaching life under the most abject genocidal conditions

For the martyrs, from every river to every sea,
especially those who died illegible deaths

For those whose queerness was erased from the pages of
history & the ancestors queered on their own terms

For our queer living, despite the systems that
attempt to annihilate Palestinians everywhere

Table of Contents:

Introduction

by George Abraham

Dear Reader,

We are writing from within the dying days of western empire and racial capital. And thus, the times are brutal: US-backed Zionist genocide spirals on in Gaza, after ceasefire after failed ceasefire, and escalates into an unnecessary, colonially expansionist war with Iran that displaces hundreds of thousands in Lebanon; and the UAE-backed genocide in Sudan continues to brutalize our kin. In the US, the domestic effects of these genocides are not merely felt; they are co-produced by the legal, carceral, and military regimes that the American settler machine has been deploying against Black and Indigenous people of all sexualities, as well as queer and trans people of all ethnicities, for generations. It is a truth Nasser Abourahme articulated in his 2024 *Radical Philosophy* essay, "In tune with their time," writing: "Colonial endgames can last a long time; they are almost always utterly brutal. But the brutality is as much a sign of their defeated denouement as much as anything else."

Contextualized within this interconnected settler genocidal regime, it is unsurprising to witness a rise of queer and trans insurgence, both globally and domestically in the US, standing in solidarity with Palestinians against the very regimes that dispose of all of our bodies without hesitation or consequence. Yes, our "post-10/7" world is scary and brutal in ways unlike anything in recorded history: permitting a live-streamed genocide is an abominable failure of humanity and dangerous precedent to set for the (failing) international order. For the first time in my own life, I have seen the tangible ways this genocidal moment is changing our community's understanding of queerness. In conversations with even the most conservative Palestinian Americans, several are starting to notice that queer and trans kin are visibly standing with Palestine in ways that put their lives and livelihoods on the line. A friend tells me that her Southern US–based, homophobic, transphobic Palestinian parents, for the first time in their lives, are starting to unlearn these harmful views because of this notable queer solidarity. *These queer siblings in the heart of empire are more our kin than any of these Khalijis, who could stop this genocide with a snap of a finger.* It's a sentence I'd never have imagined hearing from certain members of our diasporic community. It's sad that it has taken a live-streamed genocide and decades of tireless grassroots organizing and political education efforts from AlQaws, Aswat, and queer Palestinians globally, for many to have the necessary existential crises with their conceptions of *kin*. But, pessoptimistically, it is a testament to the living power of organized people, even in the face of genocidal nuclear powers armed with marketing campaigns to distract us and divide us even further from each other.

It is, thus, imperative that we examine our movements, their successes and failures, in context of longer timelines than this endless *present* within which empire wants to trap us. The strength of our free Palestine movement now, and especially of our brave student resistance that has consistently put itself at the frontlines with methods inspired by Vietnam War protests, would not be nearly as immense without the Unity Intifada of 2021, the Black Lives Matter uprisings of 2020, the Great March of Return, the

Ferguson uprisings, and the long arc of solidarity between Black and Palestinian leftist movements. Palestine, too, has learned from our radical Asian American and Pacific Islander kin, fighting the entangled domestic-foreign effects of imperial wars in contexts like Korea and Vietnam, and learning from generations of Indigenous anti-colonial insurgence from Kanaka Maoli, Maori, Samoan, and Oceania kin. We learn together with generations of people fighting US imperial intervention in Latin America—which today is putting all eyes on Cuba and Venezuela—and the long genocidal arc that racial capital's founding violence continues to inflict on the African continent. We can draw direct lines from the Transatlantic Slave Trade that founded the western economy as we know it, to the current techno-capitalist driven genocide in Congo and gold-economy driven genocide in Sudan. Taken together, it has never been clearer: the whole world is at stake in this fight against imperialism.

What, then, to say of the body at the end of empire? The fact of the global Covid-19 pandemic, which has proved, beyond domestic-international boundaries, that the ruling class is more than willing to dispose of our bodies on a mass scale for their continued profit. It is a lesson our queer and trans kin have been embodying for generations, fighting against colonial mediated bio-disposability in the AIDS pandemic. The biopolitical arc of the western world order is genocide, *disposability* via *despisability*. Palestinian and queer struggles, non-metaphorically, are interconnected at an intimate, embodied level. We are the bodies that the bio-political order paves over in its living; the permissible slaughter, however fast or slow our deaths are. We are the bodies who cannot even die coherently, as countless Palestinian and queer scholars of necropolitics have shown us. Our communities bear the embodied aftermath of what Jasbir K. Puar articulates as "the right to maim," as Gaza becomes the home of the most child amputees in the world as a result of this US–Zionist genocide. Meanwhile, domestically, state after state outlaws the basic existence of trans people (especially trans women), upholding a legal order paralleling medical apartheid against our most vulnerable queer and trans kin. In a recent talk at Mount Holyoke College, Puar reminded us that these transphobic attacks are not merely identitarian, but are in fact the ruling class's effort to *reconstitute* the gender binary, which has always been at the center of its colonial hegemony. To this, I add: what is the Zionist project if not the US's attempt to reaffirm the global permissibility of colonial domination? What are all of our bodies if not the exact targets the ruling class need to dispose of, by any means necessary, to keep the rotted heart of this current world order beating?

It is here, in the depths of our genocidal despair, carrying the embodied aftermath of several forms of interconnected imperial bio-disposability, that our community gathers in the rage and mourning we call *Homosexual Intifada*. Let us be clear: we come not to conflate queer and Palestinian struggles artificially, but to confront difficult intersections face-on with our most vulnerable kin. We come not to water down the resistance, or to say that all forms of being queer and/or Palestinian are free from capture and co-optation by the powers that be. Instead, we come to think about the ways queer and Palestinian identities might co-resist, pushing each other to bolder horizons of resistance, knowing that our entangled fight is one against an entire world order, and one that carries many universes of grief. We come with deep reverence to the concept of Intifada—Arabic for "uprising," coming from the root of "shaking off"—a word that I, myself, and many of our contributors from Palestine to the US have had our material livelihoods threatened for using, let alone, centering in our daily lives. We honor and uplift the Unity Intifada of 2021, echoing the words of the manifesto of dignity and hope: "This long Intifada is, at its heart, an Intifada of consciousness... It will stand in the face of all the elites working to deepen and entrench the divisions in and between our communities."

Editing this anthology has connected us with queer Palestinians all over the world, across generations and transnational contexts. This is one small gathering of our community, which does not aim to be definitive, but instead aims to be a conversation starter for more queer Palestinian convergences. The forms of the writing and art in this book are as varied as the material life experiences of our diverse contributors: an essay anonymously co-written with three trans women in Gaza brought to us by Afeef Nessouli, a visual poetic re-interpretation of a decades-old poem by lesbian Palestinian elder Micaela Kaibni Raen that first appeared in Interlink's historic *The Poetry of Arab Women* anthology, a classic Arabic myth queered and reimagined into the voice of a contemporary gay auntie by living Palestinian legend Randa Jarrar, and a photo essay by Al Maqdisi, asking readers to carry images of queer Palestinian bodies returning to the minute contours of our land.

I remember spending time with several of our contributors at the Palestine Writes conference in 2023, wherein several fiction- and poetry-focused panels brought up the topic of memoir being the single genre that was too much to bear head-on. As our anthology releases, amid an abundance of queer Palestinian memoir from Tareq Baconi, Randa Jarrar, and Tariq Ra'ouf (forthcoming from Interlink), it is interesting to note that among our anthology submissions, from writers emerging and established, is a fearless embrace of the facticity of our narratives. Dream journals from Elias Jahshan are placed alongside Palestinian lesbian reckonings by Noor Aldayeh and groundbreaking academic work by Sarona Abuaker reconceptualizing the queer phenomenology of Palestinian return, while one of our foremost queer Palestinian American scholars and poets, Mejdulene Bernard Shomali, breaks binaries between homeland and diaspora narratives in her lyrically searing and unforgettable memoir of queerness, heartbreak, and bodies.

There is speculative fiction by Sara Solara, who takes an interesting ecological spin with her work, and Eman Abdelhadi, who remains one of our fiercest and bravest voices, putting herself on the frontlines not merely with her words but her actions. There is poetry from international icons such as Noor Hindi, Tariq Ra'ouf, and Maria, as well as deeply personal contributions from editors Hannah Moushabeck and myself. As a whole, this anthology reminds us that our strength, as queer Palestinian writers, is in our fearless embrace of our most intimate reckonings: that in the depths of our interiors, we arrive at the most dangerous, earth-shattering questions for our collectives.

We hope these works, which treat queer Palestinian life on our own terms, give you clarity and precision of language that feels dangerous to the imperial English of our daily lives. We hope these stories and reckonings help embolden your actions towards a free Palestine, from the river to the sea, and deepen your commitments to your collectives, from every river to every sea.

With love,
George Abraham

The Fisherwoman

by Randa Jarrar

Biiiitch, let me tell you this fisherwoman story. Now, in the old days, these types of stories were told by women only, or mainly by women. When a man told them, he was considered *niswanji*, someone who preferred the company of women. An F-slur, honey. We love a storytelling queen. This shit is the type of *hikayeh* we are supposed to tell each other like late late, or with tea, or to while away the hours when under some kind of occupation. Kids can hear this story too, but I'm telling it to you the way I know how to tell stories, with profanity thrown in for no reason except because I Want to Include It.

I know some of you are scared and grieving and angry because of the fuck trash that is so-called America and Israhell, and that's okay. Sit and be held by Aunty and her story about what happened when this queer fisherwoman was once also scared, just like you.

Also, while you listen, I want you to really enjoy the fact that our people invent and tell the most badass, weirdo, out of control shit of all time.

So listen.

The fisherwoman was living by herself in a small shack near the sea, where she rode her boat every morning and cast her net in the waters. When she came back to her small shack, she butchered and fileted the fish for the market and kept two fish, always: one for herself, and one for her neighbor, the widow.

The widow felt sorry for the fisherwoman and cooked a piece of fish for her every day, and left it covered at her doorstep. And every day, the fisherwoman thanked the widow by leaving her an extra piece of fish.

No, the two were not fucking or hooking up at all—this is called community, honey. COMMUNE-TITTY. They did this for each other just to be kind.

One day, the fisherwoman came home and found that her shack had been swept clean, and her fish had been cooked in her kitchen in the most scrumptious way. She was surprised that her neighbor had come to her home uninvited, so she went to thank her. But the neighbor said that she had not come into the home, and that she would never trespass without the fisherwoman's permission. Consent, honey.

But the next two days, the same thing happened. The fisherwoman would come home to a clean shack, warm blankets and tea, and a perfectly spicy fish. The fuck?

"Girl," the widow neighbor said, "I have an idea. Why don't you stay near your window this evening instead of going to the market? I can sell the fish for you. Stay and spy and see who has been cooking you this delicious fish."

The fisherwoman agreed, and what did she spy? Three beautiful Jinni women descending from the ceiling of the shack, singing, cooking, and dancing! The fisherwoman entered her shack, shook.

The Jinnis stopped what they were doing. The Jinni the fisherwoman saw first said, "Oh shit! Now that you've seen me, I am your *qismet.*" Yeah, 'kismet' is an Arabic word. I know, right? Sadly that shit has been co-opted by fake coffee shops and chicken stalls all over the world; they love colonizing us. Anyway, the Jinni said, "My name is Khadduja, and these are my sisters." The fisherwoman greeted them all, and thanked them being so kind to her, so frequently. "You are kind to the people of your village and to your neighbors," said Khaddujah, the sister that wanted to be the fisherwoman's kismet. The fisherwoman was amazed, and asked Khaddujah so many questions. Khaddujah asked the fisherwoman about herself, too.

And so Khaddujah and the fisherwoman fell in love, had a cute little wedding, and lived by the sea.

Aunty wishes she could tell you that the fisherwoman and Khaddujah lived happily ever after, but their joy was short-lived, because why else? Men exist.

Here's what happened. One day, while Khaddujah was grilling fish and hanging clothes on the line outside the shack, the king saw her from his watchtower.

He called for the fisherwoman. She went to the king and said, "What do you want?"

"I want your wife," he said, "And I will have her. If you refuse, I will chop off your head."

"Fuck you mean?" said the fisherwoman.

"Your wife is the sexiest woman I've ever seen. If you want to keep her, then you must bring me a freshly planted grapevine to the castle door. In the morning, I want to find a single bunch of grapes on the vine, and I want this bunch to feed me and my entire army."

"That's impossible!" said the fisherwoman. "Fuck am I supposed to do that?"

"Deliver me the grapevine or deliver me your wife. If you fail to do either, I will take your head, dyke."

The fisherwoman went home and cried in Khaddujah's lap. Khaddujah said not to worry.

"Listen, *habibti*. Go to my sister's house. Call out, and her creature, who is three things and wears a small hat, will meet you with a vine. Take it to the palace doors and plant it. And leave the rest up to God."

The fisherwoman, surprised and confused, did as her wife instructed. At the sister's home, a creature that was part donkey, part gazelle, and part cat emerged from nothing, wearing a small green hat and carrying a vine in its jaws. The fisherwoman thanked the creature and took the vine to the palace doors and planted it.

The next day, the vine bore the fruit of a single bunch of grapes. The king and his men ate it all up, but the bunch still bore exactly the same amount of fruit.

"Fisherwoman!" called the king.

"What now?" said the fisherwoman.

"I still want your wife. Go find me a loaf of bread that stays hot and feeds me and my army and never gets smaller."

"Or you will chop my head?" she said.

"Or I will chop your head," the king said. "And take your woman."

Again, the fisherwoman went to Khaddujah and wept, not knowing how to appease the king, save herself, and save her love.

And again, Khaddujah said, "*Habibti*, go to the creature near my sister and ask it for the loaf of bread that sits on the kitchen ledge. Don't worry. The king will not have me, and he will not harm you."

The fisherwoman went to the sister's home and the creature emerged again, this time with a brown hat, holding a fresh and thick loaf of bread. The fisherwoman thanked the creature and took the bread to the king.

The king ate the bread with all his army, and his jesters, and his press secretaries, and his ministers of defense. No matter how much they ate, the bread loaf did not diminish.

"How dare you," the king said, "come between me and what I want! Bring me your wife."

"Girl, no," the fisherwoman said.

"Then bring me a newborn baby," said the king, "with her cord still hanging off, who tells me stories that are lies from beginning to end."

The fisherwoman went home, carrying the endless bread loaf under her arm, to Khaddujah and told her it was time to give in. The king wanted the impossible, once again. Khaddujah told the fisherwoman not to despair.

"Go to my sister," she said. "She is giving birth right now. Ask to borrow her newborn for a few moments. She won't mind."

"Are you sure?" the fisherwoman asked.

"Go," said Khaddujah, readying a horse for the fisherwoman.

The fisherwoman arrived at the sister's home just in time for the birth of a healthy baby. She took this baby to the king. The baby then began to regale the king with her own story.

She said, "I was minding my business, literally. I ran a thriving olive oil soap business from Nablus to Jenin. Throughout the plain I would travel, riding on the back of a very big hen who loved wearing lipstick and maximalist costume jewelry. I bought her any accessory she desired. Then, one day, I noticed that my hen was struggling, and a healer I found on an app told me to rub some almond oil on her back, so I did. Well, guess what? The almond oil made things much, much worse. The hen grew a massive almond tree, with huge blossoms the size of tits. I had to beg the villagers in the place where we were stopped to help me trim the tree and save my hen, but even with forty-two villagers trimming the tree, the hen could not stop sprouting.

"So I threw a clod of dirt at the tree, but what happened next was insane. The clod of dirt turned into a plain of land the size of Jerusalem. I went up to the land and saw that it was fertile and ready for planting, so I put in some sesame seeds. But then, a group of fancy-looking people in a caravan drove by and saw me and said, Sis, plant watermelons here instead. Watermelons will grow very robustly here. I listened to them and got rid of all the sesame to plant the watermelon, but there was one little sesame seed left in the mouth of an ant. I fought with that bitch for three hours, trying to pull the seed out of her tiny-ass ant mouth, and I finally won! By then, there were more than a thousand watermelons in the field.

"I took my knife out like this"—and here the baby took a knife from behind her curls—"and I chopped a watermelon open, but my knife got lost in the watermelon. I was fucking heated! I jumped in the watermelon to get it back and found myself in a marketplace butcher shop. By the time I found my knife and was about to grab it back, I felt someone tugging on me. That's when this lady brought me here. Where am I and what ... even ... is this?"

The king paused, then turned to the fisherwoman and said,

"Please get away from me and go home to your wife. I will never bother you again."

And the fisherwoman went home to her beautiful Khaddujah and this is my story, I've told it, and in your hands, I've thrown it.

Now I want you to remember, honey, that when these motherfuckers try to say they are better than us in any way, they are wrong. Because the story I just told you is an old-ass Palestinian folktale that was passed down from illiterate woman to illiterate woman until it reached me and then you. Meanwhile, white people are sitting around talking about Humpty Dumpty sitting on a wall. All the king's horses and all the king's men will never ever put Humpty together again. That bitch is broken. And they will never ever break us. Because when we fall off a wall, we rebuild the fucking wall, tiny little stone by stone. We call it *salsilling* the wall in Arabic. We invented that shit. And if we do fall off the wall and break, we go inside our broken pieces and find a marketplace and a butcher shop and a farming field and a caravan in that shit. We are entire worlds, bitch. So fuck these monstrous foul-smelling empires and fuck what they think they can do to us. We will never be erased. We will never be stolen from each other. We will continue to drive the king crazy, while the king thinks he can ask the impossible of us. The fisherwoman and her wife remind us that nothing is impossible, and that we are goddamn magic, and they know it, and we know it, and never ever will we end.

Arab Lesbianism Is Not an Oxymoron[1]

by Noor Aldayeh

In my senior year of undergrad, I watched Nadine Naber's TedTalk, "Arab Feminism is Not an Oxymoron," for one of my Women's, Gender, and Sexuality Studies courses. Naber discusses the disappointing and narrow discourse granted to women of Southwest Asia and North Africa (SWANA) in discussions of "Arab feminism." She points out the Orientalist and Islamophobic norms often fraught in viewing of the diverse cultures, ethnicities, religions, and regions that make up the SWANA world as a homogenized "Arab and Muslim" front, rather than acknowledging the full range and complexities of SWANA and the feminist movements within it.

She details the rich history of women's participation in liberation movements across the SWANA world, specifically citing that 40 percent to 50 percent of protesters in the 2011 Tahrir Square demonstrations in Egypt were women, (as well as mentioning that feminist groups have existed there since the 1920s). She also notes dismissive discourse surrounding "the Veil" as it relates to white, second-wave feminism; the failure to address systemic discrimination against SWANA/

1 Title inspired by Nadine Naber's "Arab Feminism is Not an Oxymoron"

Muslim peoples in a post 9/11 society, such as targeted government surveillance and repeated attacks against individuals and groups of this background; the cognitive dissonance of Western perspectives regarding human rights in parts of the world we have direct hands in disenfranchising.

Naber states poignantly in her talk, "Why are we so eager to accept the idea of a backwards foreign culture that oppresses women? Is it because that's easier than confronting the very devastating impact the US war on terror has had on women in countries like Iraq?" She adds, "And when are feminists in the US going to start to define war as a form of violence against women?"

What Naber articulates so clearly in this speech represents a framework that I argue could be applied to many concepts regarding Western-versus-non-Western discourse and understandings of identity, culture, and the fight towards collective liberation. As a nonbinary Syrian-Palestinian lesbian who was born and raised in the West, I have been forced to come to terms with this exact tension within my identity.

It is this tension that I also hope to name and challenge as it applies to queer liberation in the SWANA world, most especially as it has do with lesbianism and transness. This is not to deny that the same is true of queer cis men in some capacities; I am merely stating that this is not the focus of this piece.

I have chosen to focus on lesbians and gender-nonconforming peoples (GNC) for the same reason Naber titled her speech "Arab Feminism is Not an Oxymoron." In the West, decades of propaganda has resulted in overarching notions and stereotypes of the SWANA world as one that is uniquely terrible to women and downright murderous to the queer community, though discussions of these issues often center on cis gay men without any acknowledgement of lesbians, GNC, or other queer experiences.

It has become a common talking point to imply that queer folks fighting for collective liberation in SWANA are acting counterintuitively. Ignoring the fact that we should fight for what is right regardless of whether or not one accepts our identity, these arguments often throw homo- and transphobia in our faces, to say that we would be murdered if we were to exist as queer and trans people in the SWANA world.

Many of these misplaced notions have emerged due to the sensationalistic way events regarding homophobia in the SWANA region are portrayed in the media. Horrific tales of violence and killing of queer individuals are written about at length and spread far and wide, while our nuanced lives, histories, and participation in the fight towards liberation are actively erased, censored, and ignored.

Though they are presenting themselves as advocates for the LGBTQ community, those who spew these arguments rarely ever acknowledge that queer and trans folks already live in these places, in and out of the closet, fighting for their liberation in various capacities. They also often ignore their own perpetuation of hatred, via their expression of racist, aggressive, and violent intent to the queer people they are criticizing.

Fascinatingly (note the sarcasm here), the state of homo/transphobia in the West is often left unmentioned in this discourse. Many of these sensationalized stories take on the tone of "Look at those crazy homophobic Arabs who would do anything they want to gay people! Thank God we're not like that here in the safe and accepting West, where nothing ever happens to queer folks!"

To deny that misogyny and homo/transphobia exist in the SWANA world would simply be false, but to present these structures as inherently "more evil" within non-Western contexts is harmful, unproductive, and downright inaccurate. It is rooted in clear bigotry and the inherent belief that we in the West are superior to our non-Western counterparts. Especially in the wake of America's current mask-off spiral into fascism (a route it has been on arguably since its inception), the attack on BIPOC, LGBTQ+ existences and histories is increasingly palpable and concerning.

Additionally, as pointed out by Naber, to dilute arguments about queer liberation in the SWANA world as solely freeing queer SWANA individuals from a "Big Bad Arab Monster" ignores the true enemy: decades of destruction, violence, genocide, and societal disenfranchisement, imposed at every level on the SWANA world by Western imperialism and colonialism. It is a distraction from the true issues faced by marginalized communities—and another form of discrimination as we prescribe to them what we feel their freedom should look like.

Most frustratingly so as it pertains to queerness in particular—these diluted arguments ignore the most vital acknowledgement of all: that the invention of homophobia is an inherently Western, colonialist ideal that was forced upon the SWANA world, as well as many, if not most, non-Western cultures affected by colonialism/imperialism. It is perversely ironic that most of the communities being forced to answer for homophobia had nothing to do with its existence in the first place. Again, these people are often dealing with the far more pressing issue of their own daily survival.

An excerpt from "From Pinkwashing to Pinkwatching: Palestinian Queer Resistance" by Nelly Bassily:

> So we are saying that not only should we be countering Israel's project of occupation and Apartheid but we should also counter it because it is based on a racist, colonial logic. So, we are saying that if this racist, colonial logic makes a lot of sense to LGBT communities in North America and Europe, it says a lot about them and their willingness to overlook facts. And, pinkwashing as a propaganda tool is unfortunately smart. It speaks the language that others want to hear. It integrates islamophobia and anti-Arab concepts and this false binary of modern vs. backward that has been promoted in LGBT communities and then pinkwashing comes and popularizes these notions. If you follow this logic, Israel is being promoted as this amazing place with white, sandy beaches and hot guys while completely ignoring that these same hot guys that LGBT people come to Israel and dance with in Tel Aviv parties are the same hot guys who are soldiers and killing kids in different neighbourhoods in Palestine. That's the really horrifying logic behind pinkwashing.
>
> Also, pinkwashing is an insidious colonial violence on queer bodies in Palestine because it works to strengthen myths about Palestine. It is telling a lot of queer Palestinians who are struggling with a lot of oppression and homophobia, as any queer person is,

> that they could be saved by their colonizer. Pinkwashing sells to Palestinian queers this fantasy that their colonizer has their freedom while holding their freedom, making young queers dream about Tel Aviv and about moving to Israel, while in fact they can't cross over because it is illegal for Palestinians living within '67 borders and Gaza to be inside Israel, and that is a direct violence on queer Palestinians. The other thing pinkwashing does is push LGBT Palestinians to hate their families and society and alienates them by peddling this false notion that their families and their society have no hope of recovering from this "disease" called homophobia. This impedes the efforts of progressive forces in Palestine that work to change attitudes and work with families.

For those of us not fully brushed up on the history of sexuality and gender—the binary view of both originated in Victorian-era England*, where for the first time, gender roles and expectations were created, adopted, and normalized in society. Whereas sexuality had previously been viewed more in terms of power dynamics—often through the lens of the penetrated versus the penetrator than between male and female—this newly invented "proper" marital/nuclear familial structure was subsequently enforced upon all societies affected by colonialism.

From "Penetration and Its Discontents: Greco-Roman Sexuality, The Acts of Paul and Thecla and Theorizing Eros Without the Wound" by Maia Kotrosits:

> Ancient constructions of sexuality, it has been generally thought, hinged not on the gender of the person with whom you had sex but rather on what position one occupied in the sexual act: penetrator or penetrated. Indeed penetration, and concomitant notions of active and passive, structured not only ancient senses of selfhood, but also, by metonymic implication, social relations at large.

As someone deeply passionate about queer history, culture, and preservation, I've noticed that this acknowledgement is often conveniently left out by so-called activists who are quick to label the SWANA world as uniquely unsafe for queer folks. The reality is, navigating queerness in these contexts means fighting against and actively dealing with the reality of Western violence, occupation, apartheid, colonialism, and imperialism—all of which present particularly monumental difficulties for folks existing at the intersection of multiple marginalized identities.

Again, this is not to deny that some of these structures were not present or adopted by and perpetuated within our cultures, or to say that every region within SWANA is dealing with the these struggles to the same degree. This is only to emphasize the importance of recognizing their origins, and therefore, what dismantling them would then entail: the destruction of the Empire and its practices as a whole.

Queer folks have always been and will remain at the forefront of liberation movements, whether their participation is known explicitly or not, and this is true of the SWANA world. For example, the current Free Palestine movement is in itself a fight for feminist and queer liberation—because true collective liberation includes freedom and justice for ALL. Queer individuals, feminists, and allies on the ground have reiterated that their fight is decolonial and antifascist, a fight for total liberation from oppressive structures in which they have persevered both within and beyond their own communities.

As beautifully articulated in "A Liberatory Demand from Queers in Palestine" by a group called Queers in Palestine:

> "We refuse the instrumentalization of our queerness, our bodies, and the violence we face as queer people to demonize and dehumanize our communities, especially in service of imperial and genocidal acts. We refuse that Palestinian sexuality and Palestinian attitudes towards diverse sexualities become parameters for assigning humanity to any colonized society. We deserve life because we are human, with the multitude of our imperfections, and not because of our proximity to colonial modes of liberal humanity. We refuse colonial and imperialist tactics that seek to alienate us from our society and alienate our society from us, on the basis of our queerness. We are fighting interconnected systems of oppression, including patriarchy and capitalism, and our dreams of autonomy, community, and liberation are inherently tied to our desire for self-determination. No queer liberation can be achieved with settler-colonization, and no queer solidarity can be fostered if it stands blind to the racialized, capitalist, fascist, and imperial structures that dominate us."

As articulated by the collective of Black feminists who wrote "The Combahee River Collective Statement" in 1977, because Black women in America have been forced to exist at the bottom of the social hierarchy, their total liberation would necessitate that all other marginalized peoples be free. The same goes for queer and trans Palestinians in Palestine; true Palestinian liberation necessitates that Palestinian women, queer, and trans folks are free from all structures of oppression.

It is again important to acknowledge that the SWANA world is a vast and diverse region made up of dozens of unique cultures, peoples, and of course, struggles. What a queer or trans person is dealing with in Palestine may vary from what a queer or trans person is dealing with in Sudan, which may vary from what a queer or trans person is dealing with in Saudi Arabia, and so on. Many of our struggles are similar, and all of them are of course connected as aspects of the same fight towards collective liberation—but it is important that we do not make the mistake of Orientalizing our varied lived experiences in these discussions.

Similarly, within the queer community of SWANA diaspora there exists a range of unique experiences around the world, each dealing with nuanced layers of the cultures in which they have come to reside, the culture of their specific SWANA identities, and their specific queer/trans identity, all in one. When I write a piece like this, I am keenly aware of the reality that no one person can speak of or for this existence in full, and I will never claim to do this.

That said, it would be tedious, and nearly impossible, to articulate all of the particular cultural nuances present in every facet and discussion about queerness in SWANA, so we are left with doing our best with the perspectives and resources available to us. Seeing as the examples of queer history I cite often come from places where I've lived, and knowing that there are so many more stories to be told and struggles being faced throughout the SWANA region, I feel it's important to note this reality. May they all receive the visibility and respect they deserve.

Returning to discussions of feminism, it is important to acknowledge the deeply patriarchal structures present throughout the SWANA world, and see that they existed in pre-colonial contexts, although in a different fashion than they exist today. As an AFAB (assigned female at birth) person from this culture, it is frustrating to see the erasure of countless efforts towards gender liberation in SWANA by those in the West—which brings us back to Naber's Arab feminism arguments.

When queerness is discussed in the SWANA world, whether internally or externally, the effects of the patriarchy that Naber calls out remain pervasive, often resulting in queer SWANA discourse, academia, and representation centering and amplifying the (majority cis) queer male experience. SWANA lesbians and GNC individuals are often left out of interviews, articles, studies, and images of queer SWANA folks. Our lives, loves, and contributions to the world are seldom amplified or given a spotlight.

Annoyingly, when I have brought myself to queer SWANA spaces in New York City, I have still felt some level of ostracization, depending on the space, due to my gender and sexuality, and have had many conversations with others who feel similarly. Without a doubt I've been blessed with many amazing experiences and will hopefully have more in the future, but what I'm trying to articulate here is a deeper systemic issue that many queer BIPOC women and GNC deal with daily in our communities.

Though the limited, bigoted, and largely biased state of our representation would have one think otherwise, the lesbian identity has a long documented history in the SWANA world, one that originated 400 years prior to the first documentation of queer SWANA men. Again, sources dedicated *solely* to folks of our identity are few and far between, yet there have been consistent efforts within our communities for increased SWANA lesbian and GNC visibility, academia, storytelling, and preservation.

As a volunteer at the Lesbian Herstory Archives in Brooklyn, New York, focusing on this type of SWANA archiving, I've spent countless hours of my life thinking about and trying to preserve queer SWANA history, in historic, present, and future tenses. I have witnessed firsthand in my work just how prevalent our existences have been throughout documented history and how much effort is put into its dismissal.

If you go digging, you'll find countless stories of ancient and medieval lesbians in SWANA, which are revered as true forms of devotion, passion, and love. Unfortunately, many of these sources are written by or from the perspective of men, and thus can suffer from heavy bouts of oversexualization and invalidation of our identities.

"Medieval Arab Lesbians and Lesbian-Like Women" by Sahar Amer:

> The earliest extant erotic treatise in Arabic, Jawami 'al-ladhdha (Encyclopedia of Pleasure), dates to about the end of the tenth century and was written by a certain Abul Hasan Ali ibn Nasr al-Katib.' It tells us the story of the first lesbian couple, the enduring love between Hind Bint al- Nu'man, the Christian

daughter of the last Lakhmid king of Hira in the seventh century, and Hind Bint al-Khuss al-Iyadiyyah from Yamama in Arabia, known as al-Zarqa' and reportedly the first lesbian in Arab history:

> She [Hind] was so loyal to al-Zarqa' that when the latter died, she cropped her hair, wore black clothes, rejected worldly pleasures, vowed to God that she would lead an ascetic life until she passed away and, as a result, she built a monastery which was named after her, on the outskirts of Kufa. When she died, she was buried at the monastery gate. Her loyalty was then an example for poets to write about. There are also other women who continued to shed tears on their beloved ones' graves until they passed away.

Similarly, gender diversity (and what we might define as genderqueerness or transness, acknowledging such labeling as inherently colonial in nature) has an even wider and deeper standing within our history. From intersex ancient deities (see: Astarte) to gender-nonconforming djinn, to medieval androgyny to "cross-dressing," AFABs in early-1900s Egypt, Palestine, and Lebanon—beyond binary ideas and manifestations of identities—not only exist but are deeply integral to SWANA history as a whole.

Unsurprisingly, there is also documentation of the purposeful erasure and destruction of art, stories, and histories of queer SWANA women and GNC in particular (especially from sources made by folks from our identity), either due to the rise in religious conservatism in SWANA (across many faiths) or by those colonial and imperialist powers that seek to destroy our existences as a whole. Specific destructive attacks on libraries, archives, and schools/universities in countries like Palestine are an active arm of the genocide and cultural erasure of our peoples. Of course, these attacks have a profound impact on the preservation of intersectional identities and histories in our cultures.

Contemporary sources and media about SWANA lesbians and GNC very much exist and are still being produced, though they often focus on discussing the necessity of their own existence due to how few sources on this topic are accessible to the world. I have read the work of many SWANA lesbians or GNC who are speaking solely about how erased or invalidated our identities are. Many note the difficulties involved in researching, writing, or publishing the very words I was reading, for any number of social/systemic reasons. Though all of this tragically remains true, I admit that I've been craving more. More of our lived experiences, talents, deeply validating histories, and highlights of our achievements. More love stories and art pieces and characters and movies. More ... well, everything!

To this day, finding, creating, discussing, or otherwise focusing on queer SWANA sources, especially lesbian and GNC, remains a formidable task. These barriers present unique challenges to an already intersectional identity, adding in accessibility and visibility concerns that often involve an element of class status. Those who have access to higher education institutions with research databases, for example, are more likely to find and engage with sources than someone who does not. Or, for another example, it takes a great deal of financial and physical stability to have space and time to focus on these subjects when one is actively concerned with day-to-day survival.

Similarly, living in larger metropolitan cities like Los Angeles or New York, where LGBTQ histories and existences are more visible, accessible, and maintained (again, still acknowledging that homo/transphobia is rife in these areas) allows for further access and engagement with our stories. These cities are incredibly expensive to live in and not a feasible option for any number of reasons for countless individuals.

This reality means that a majority of queer SWANA stories known to the world come from the West in some capacity, or from sources not actively having to deal with on-the-ground SWANA struggles. I myself exemplify this reality. My parents are immigrants from Syria and Palestine. Had I been born in one of those areas, I would be living a drastically different life. Being born and raised in America has allowed me an acceptance and visibility of my identity that many of my peers are not afforded. Culturally, many queer SWANA folks even in the West are still not able to be out for any number of reasons, often making life with this identity feel incredibly isolating.

As someone who has only borne witness to a small fraction of this progression in the last few years, I find it heartening that there has been exponential growth in our public, global, documented existences and experiences. Social media and the internet have been pivotal in these matters, allowing for international access to sources by and about people of our identity. Additionally, as has always been true throughout history, underground communities exist and are doing immeasurable amounts of work for folks within our communities and for our movements as a whole.

Having started an ongoing ethnographic work about this identity myself in 2022, titled "Hayati: My Life / My Love; A queer Middle Eastern and North African archive," I have had the honor of meeting dozens of queer and trans folks from our background in the last couple of years. Time and time again, I have seen firsthand how folks of our identities, whether out or not, remain at the front lines of participating in vital work needed for collective liberation, in and outside of the West, across a variety of battles.

And though I have spent much of this work focused on sources and media by and about our identity, I feel it also important to note that that is not all we are. One's value is not determined by how much proof there is of your existence. Nor is it determined by how much power you have as an identity in respect to other groups in this hugely unjust world. I'd argue that one's value is determined by oneself, built upon by all those who are in community with you, and all of those who came before you and are to come.

SWANA lesbians and GNC are everywhere, doing everything. We have been around since some of the earliest known civilizations. We are your neighbors, friends, family, and loved ones. We exist in infinite realities, in infinite unique bodies. Our ancestors fearlessly blazed the trail for us in so many ways, and we have continued their legacy in resisting and persevering amid a lifetime of tribulations. We find one another and love one another and protect one another in as many ways we know how.

There are many privileges I have and sacrifices I have made in order to live the way I do as someone of my specific background. And it is due to this specific position that I find it important to discuss queer SWANA women and GNC issues more explicitly. To acknowledge our existence for the deeply rich, historic, natural, all-encompassing picture that it is. To name our identity as anything but an oxymoron, or a shameful label destined to exist perpetually in shadow.

Nothing that I have said in this piece is new in any way. But it is my firm belief that in time, we will continue to unearth more of our histories and tales of existences, to find new ways to amplify and create all of the resources and stories by, about, and for us that we deserve. Most importantly, to create a world in which we are able to live freely in our full truths, outside of any systems of oppression.

I am only able to write this now because I am not actively having to deal with the lived realities of colonialism, imperialism, apartheid, and genocide that are at this very moment being experienced in the places I am originally from. I am privileged enough to live in a major Western city where I can do the work and study the subjects of my own choosing. While I am in many ways involved in and concerned with the dismantling of these structures in the West, it is my responsibility to acknowledge the differences in my reality versus that of my queer siblings in SWANA and here.

Everything I do is for and in honor of all of the work you are not able to see, done by folks of our identity, by those who have carved the path I walk upon now and all of those who are to follow. I hope that one day, all those who want and deserve recognition, celebration, and preservation of their lives are able to experience them in full. Until then, our fights will continue in the plethora of ways they are now until total freedom is achieved.

Arab lesbianism is not an oxymoron; it never has been and never will be. Long live the intifada. Long live the resistance, and glory to all of our martyrs.

Sources:

1. Nadine Naber, "Arab Feminism is Not an Oxymoron," TedTalk (2020). https://www.youtube.com/watch?v=s_oqa3DNDZw
2. Queers in Palestine, "A Liberatory Demand from Queers in Palestine," (2023)
   a. Queers in Palestine, queersinpalestine.noblogs.org/post/2023/11/08/87/
   b. Number of signatories (523). Updated on Nov. 6, 2023,12:19 AM (Eastern European Time).
3. "The Combahee River Collective Statement" (1977)
   a. https://americanstudies.yale.edu/sites/default/files/files/Keyword%20Coalition_Readings.pdf
4. Sahar Amer, "Noor's Notes on: "Medieval Arab Lesbians and Lesbian-Like Women" (2009). (2024)
   a. nooraldayeh.substack.com/p/noors-notes-on-medieval-arab-lesbians
5. National Public Radio, All Things Considered, "The Diesel" (2012)
   a. www.npr.org/2012/07/23/157248915/review-the-diesel
6. "Cross-Dressing in Photographs of 1920s and 1930s Egypt, Palestine and Lebanon" (2013)
   a. docslib.org/doc/11166524/cross-dressing-in-photographs-of-1920 s-and-1930s-egypt-palestine-and-lebanon
7. Librarians and Archivists with Palestine, "Israeli Damage to Archives, Libraries, and Museums in Gaza, October 2023–January 2024" (2023–24)
   a. Link: https://librarianswithpalestine.org/gaza-report-2024/
8. Samar Habib, "Female Homosexuality in the Middle East" (2007) a. www.taylorfrancis.com/books/mono/10.4324/97802039414 54/female-homosexuality-middle-east-samar-habib

9 Mejdulene Bernard Shomali, "Between Banat: Queer Arab Critique and Transnational Arab Archives" (2023)
   a. www.dukeupress.edu/between-banat
10. Hayati, Noor Aldayeh (2022–ongoing)
   a. noor.aldayeh.com/hayati/

Baptize Me Anew in the Name of June Jordan

by Nadia Shammas

I confess!

Love is a limp thing
In cowardly hands
In weak hands
pneumatic joints aching wrists diseases of Kings-

I'm tired of talking the talk.

*

Meet me, instead, in the cool water
sweet and up to our knees.
Make sure there is life in it.
There is no need to check for death - it will be there
waiting under anything that moves, or might.
We watch for the distinction

This is a waste, says guilt
This is the point, says the other

*

Wondrous June, I am stained by my weakness-
I fear *pain.*
My impotent limbs flinch away from
the comforts of a clean lance.
My cowardice, overflowing, seeps from my body
black blood pooling into dams
beneath my thin skin until bursting
stinking thickly through the gaps of my teeth.

If I wrote a poem, would my words hold water?

Because
I dream of waves I want to scream
obvious
and looming, towering and crashing
all in real time.
I want to wield rage forcefully despite my feeble grip
I wish you could meet me here instead
the nowhereland of my heart
the wasteland of my intentions

The refrain - what if I am unworthy of our martyrs?
The chorus - Narcissus navel-gazing makes it so.

*

I pray!

Boil me anew in your wrath, June!
I have felt the miracle in your words
I have seen it with mine own eyes-
there is nothing sacred about fear.

Baptise me within the squall of your ferocity, and I
Will not be passive in salvation, I
Will make sacrament of my enemies, defeated, bleating, I
Will bring back the old ways!

I will remain clarified in the scalding purity
only a wretch could withstand.

Palestinian Dreaming

by Elias Jahshan

Let me tell you about a few dreams I've had.

No, not dream in the sense of goals you want to achieve. I mean *actual* dreams. The stuff that plays out in your mind while you're fast asleep. Most people would dismiss them, they'd say there are no real meanings behind your dreams. That your subconscious isn't really trying to tell you anything.

My mum would beg to differ. She is not an expert, but she somehow knows what types of dreams mean or their underlying message. I am not religious, but I do believe her dream interpretations. Telling her about a dream I had often comes up in our weekly FaceTime calls. Dreaming of a snake attacking you apparently means there is a toxic person in your life, and dreams of teeth falling out can be associated with death, particularly the death of a loved one. But dreaming of attending the funeral of a loved one who is still alive somehow means you have just prolonged their life.

In my late thirties, I suddenly lost what remained of my hearing, with the hearing aids I relied on my whole life no longer being able to help me. Around this time, I dreamt of driving the car with my husband in the passenger seat, where we'd be talking and suddenly I'd shush him as I turned up the volume on a song I loved. My mum said it was a sign of things to come. She was right: getting my cochlear implant meant I could enjoy music again after a year of near-complete silence. It changed my life.

But there are two other powerful dreams I had that were so vivid, they have stayed with me years since I awoke from them. Let me start with the first dream. This is how it went.

It's set in the dining room of my old house in Dundas, in Sydney's western suburbs. The whole family is gathered around the table for a feast. My brother and his wife, my older sister and her husband, my brother's three kids, my sister's three kids, my other sister, my mum, and my late dad.

The table was bare, the thick plastic tablecloth covering the oversized doily making it look squeaky clean. The room was so bright—a blinding whiteness that obscures faces and other little details. I recall the dining room window, its bleached white net curtains billowing from a slight breeze, but I couldn't see the cabinets where Mum kept her cherished family photos on display. I could feel the tiled floors, but they were covered in what appeared to be fluffy clouds. Is this what the dining room would be like in heaven? There was an undeniable, ethereal warmth about it. Maybe because a dining room is the heart and soul of the home.

I remember everyone laughing, having a good time. I don't remember what the topic of discussion was. This isn't one of those dreams where you recall what was said. But I remember Dad sitting at his usual spot on the dining table with a warm smile on his face. He was not looking at me or anyone else in particular. He was not laughing his usual wheezy, infectious laugh as he regaled us with a joke or a story about Palestine. He was just sitting there, looking serenely at peace. This dream came to me several months after he passed away. I remember feeling a sense of bittersweet joy. Maybe it's because Dad was surrounded by the whole family. His family.

Mum was sitting right next to him, hugging his right arm and laying her head on his shoulder. She was never really big on PDAs in real life, but they did hold hands in public from time to time, and she loved it when Dad showered her with love. But in this dream, she just wouldn't let go, even while deep in buoyant conversation with the family, her animated hand gestures making her seem more Lebanese than usual. It looked as if she would be happy to remain clasped to his side.

She did do that in real life, at least. Especially in his final weeks in hospital. I have vivid memories of Oum Kalthoum's "Enta Omri" playing on a laptop beside Dad's deathbed, his eyes closed and hand moving along with the iconic string arrangements, while Mum kisses him on the forehead, her cheeks moist with tears. Dad passed away a few days later, just one month shy of their fortieth wedding anniversary. The memories of the love they had for each other is something I always think of fondly.

I don't know what that dream means and I haven't even told Mum about it, not in the seventeen years since Dad's passing. I don't know if I can bring myself to. Writing about it is easier.

Maybe the dream was Dad's way of telling me he was content and at peace, wherever his soul went to rest. Perhaps it was a message that he will always love his whole family, the home he created for himself as a Palestinian in exile. Maybe it was a way to reassure me that he would always watch over us, especially his six grandchildren, who all grow up to contribute—in their own ways—to the cacophony of sounds that come with family gatherings and feasts around the same dining table.

Maybe it was to show me that Mum will always be his soul mate, and vice versa. She may have stopped wearing black after the first six months of mourning, but seventeen years later, she still grieves for Dad. She will never shake off that grief. She has made space for it in her life, whether she realizes it or not. At least this means she lives with his memories and his love.

Dad was also loved, respected, and admired by so many—not just the family, or relatives, but also among Sydney's Palestinian and wider Arab community. My siblings and I nicknamed him "the godfather" because of how some relatives often turned to him for help on matters pertaining to Australian bureaucracy (Dad was the most fluent in English of his generation) or for advice on resolving family feuds. People were always delighted by his warm and calming presence. He could also command a room with his natural public speaking talent. His hospitality was the stuff of legend, and his ability to make you smile a symbol of his jovial, kind soul. He always found a way to insert a hilarious joke at the perfect moment in any situation, even when he was on his deathbed. I remember when an Orthodox priest visited the hospital to give him his last rites, and after he left Dad had everyone in fits of giggles after he poked fun at the pompous manner he administered the rites. He always said laughter was the best medicine for anything, even during times of sadness.

Just like every Palestinian, Dad loved life, and he taught us to love life too. Maybe that's why his passing affected me so much, why I still write about it all these years later. I was twenty-three when he died—just finished university, my whole life ahead of me. Maybe that dream of the bright dining room was a manifestation of the early stages of my grief: mourning the fact I would never have the chance to talk to him about my ambitions again, to just have a laugh about something (as we were wont to do), or to talk about politics—especially when it comes to Palestine.

Since then, I sometimes lament how he never had the chance to see me shake off the teenage angst that plagued me into my early twenties to embrace my culture and become a proud Palestinian, just like he was. I feel sad about never having the chance to share my published articles about Palestine with him, or my books on queer Arabs, or my other writings. He missed out on meeting Aaron, the person who would become my husband. Most of all, he missed seeing how my intersectional identity would become my superpower, informing my radical politics and desire for equality, equity and justice.

Perhaps that's why he was just so happy just sitting there in the dream. All my anxieties over my Palestinian identity would soon be overcome. All my fears about him not accepting me for being gay, they were all unfounded after all, even after the homophobic remarks he sometimes made about other gay men while I was growing up. It makes me wonder if he visited me in my dream to show me that he would've always loved me as his son, regardless. I could be reaching, or even projecting. Does it matter, though?

***

That dream of the bright dining room happened only once, but its details are seared into my memory. The exact same thing can be said of the second dream I'm about to tell you, which happened more than a decade later. This is how it went.

This one came probably about twelve years after Dad's passing. I was living in London at this point, and the dream happened at the peak of the Covid pandemic, when vaccines were finally being rolled out but travel was still a no-go with borders being shut. I know this because it was several months after Ummo Ibrahim passed away. He wasn't my uncle in the traditional sense, but as the husband of Amto Fortoneh—my paternal aunt and godmother—he was like a second father to me, so I called him Ummoh out of respect. Not being able to fly to Australia to attend his funeral, to mourn with family, was gut-wrenching.

When I spoke about this dream with Mum over FaceTime, she cried. As did Amto Fortoneh, who happens to be my dad's only sibling. Similar to the first dream, the setting of this one is my old house in Dundas. But this time it's outside, in the front yard. It didn't have that ethereal element of the first dream, but it was still bright. In fact it was a stunning summer's day with blue skies and not a single cloud. Not humid, but not stiflingly hot like it often gets over summer in Sydney. The house is a single-story, post-World War II ex-housing commission fibro build that's been rendered over with concrete to give it a fresh look, with red terracotta roof tiles and ringed by a beautiful rose garden which Mum meticulously tends to.

I can see the huge concrete slab that goes from the footpath down to the gate that leads to the backyard. You can easily park about four cars on that driveway, three back-to-back and another on the little bit of concrete that juts out to the side by the small patch of lawn and the front porch. But there were no cars on the driveway in this dream, and the small patch of lawn was draped in the shadow of a huge pine tree that used to dominate the front yard. Before I moved to London, that tree had to be cut down. The roots were causing issues to the foundation of the house, but it was a gorgeous tree. Mum would always say it reminded her of the cedars of Lebanon.

On the lower part of the driveway, branches of a jacaranda tree from next door loom over it, the vivid purple flowers in full bloom. Under the shade of this spectacular tree is a really long table, one that fits about thirty people. It's not just the immediate family present this time. Everyone from Amto's side of the family is gathered around. So are my two cousins, their spouses, and kids. Amto herself and Ummo Ibrahim are there too.

This was actually the first and only time I had ever dreamt of him and my old man together after they had both passed away. As with the other dream, I don't remember why we were all there. It was a big feast, of course, I remember a massive spread of food. There was kibbeh bil souniyeh, there was djaj that'd been marinated and baked with toum, hashwet rouz decorated with toasted almond slivers, waraq dawali with koussa mahshi, lahme and kifta on skewers fresh from the charcoal barbecue, and even my favorite: laban immo. There was arak too. Dad and Ummo were drinking some of that stuff. I am pretty sure Amto took a cheeky sip from Ummo's glass, as she sometimes did in real life.

There was lively conversation, as usual. I don't recall making eye contact with or speaking to Dad or Ummo. But I do remember Mum and Amto both being happy—as if they had both been reunited with their beloved husbands. My siblings, niblings, cousins, and I were also happy. Everyone was living life to the fullest.

But this dream had an important detail. I recall the main window by the front porch of the house being wide open like a kiosk. Behind it was Tata Victoria. This was the first and only time I had ever dreamt of her. Mum thought this was eerie, as we had never met. Tata Victoria, my dad and Amto's mother, died three years before I was born.

I knew everyone had been eating dessert, warbat, but it all ran out. I knew Tata was the one who made them—and the whole feast. But it didn't seem odd that she just remained in the house, not joining us on the long table under the jacaranda tree. I got up to go to the front window to ask her if she made any more. But Tata refused to give me anything, let alone look me in the eye. She turned away from me and gesticulated as if to say "no." I never made eye contact with her; all I saw were snatches of her profile and the back of most of her head, the permed, gray curls ringing the base of her bobbed hair style.

Mum wasn't sure what this dream meant as a whole, but she was relieved that Tata rejected my request for more dessert at least. Otherwise it would spell a bad omen in my reality. Members of the dead taking or giving things to you, still living, is essentially bad luck. While it was reassuring that I should not expect to face a negative turn of events in my life anytime soon, it was also a bit disheartening. I hear so much about my grandmother, especially via my siblings, who are all older and have fond childhood memories involving her. I felt this dream was as close I could've ever come to meeting her, my only chance to chat with her and ask all my burning questions. But it wasn't to be.

I'm not exactly sure why I remember this dream so vividly. Maybe my subconscious was reminding me to make the most of the time I had left with the few Palestinian elders in my family who were still alive. Elders who had endured the 1948 Nakba as children or teenagers, whose collective traumatic experiences have informed me and my desire for justice—and radical love—for my people. My father was nine and a half years old when Tata, fearing for her family's safety, decided to flee their seaside Yaffa home amid news of an imminent invasion from Zionist forces in May 1948. Even as they joined the Palestinian exodus to stay with relatives in Ramallah, Tata was convinced it would only be temporary, as they barely had time to pack enough clothes. She thought they'd be able to return once the fighting was over. But they were banned from ever doing so; the Zionists made sure of that.

Years later, Tata would up her life again to follow her two children—now adults—to the other side of the world, to watch them marry and establish their own families. Meanwhile in Yaffa, the sandstone home in the Ajami neighborhood that she shared with two of her brothers and their respective families was erased from history. No one knows exactly when the house was demolished, but Zionist settlers transformed the vicinity into a landfill before eventually building an artificial park on top of it that buried swathes of Ajami's shoreline. The streets were renamed in Hebrew, erasing its Palestinian past, but at least the nearby Hassan Arafeh mosque survived. Tata also never had the chance to see the grave of her husband, my Siddo George, ever again. I tried to locate it when I went to visit in 2011, but it wasn't possible. All pre-1948 documentation of the graves had been lost, likely destroyed by Zionists after the 1948 invasion. It saddens me that Siddo's tombstone, somewhere in an Orthodox cemetery in Yaffa that overlooks the Mediterranean, has faded into obscurity.

My father was among the youngest in his generation. Around the time of my feast dream in the front yard, only two elders remained alive: Amto and Ummo Abdo, my dad's closest cousin in age. Ummo Abdo was also my godfather. Every other Nakba-surviving elder in my family—at least those who came from Yaffa and made Sydney their home—had passed away at that point. But within a year after this dream, Ummo Abdo also passed away, and around nine months later, so did Amto.

I cannot begin to describe the regret I carry from not taking the time to properly speak to and learn from my elders about the Yaffa of their childhood, their Nakba memories, their early years of exile in Amman, and the challenges of putting down roots in Sydney. Maybe that's why Tata would not look me in the eye; she could well have been disappointed that I didn't try hard enough to glean their stories. I'm supposed to be the writer in the family, after all.

There's much symbolism behind the vivid imagery of this dream, though. Jacarandas and pine trees are not native to Australia; both are introduced species of trees. Just as my family is not indigenous to the land. And the fact that we were gathered in this space, enjoying each other's company and a sumptuous feast with Tata in the background—it's almost as if the message is that we are all the fruits of her labor. From Yaffa to Sydney, her recipes sustain and nurture us, and always bring us together as a family. The food is a clear reminder of our Palestinian-ness, and how it transcends generations. Cooking and feeding loved ones was also Tata's love language, one that I, my siblings, and cousins have all inherited.

It may seem strange that Siddo wasn't in this dream, but the truth is that even my father and Amto never really dreamt of him. He died when they were just nine months and two years old, respectively. I regret never having the chance to ask either of them if Tata ever dreamt of him. I'm sure she did.

***

My husband, Aaron, was not in that feast dream either. After all, we were married by that point. But at least he's in the next dream. Only that wasn't an actual dream. It's a daydream, and one I have often. This daydream came together in my mind shortly after Amto's passing, two and a half years ago. This is how it goes.

She was like a second mother, and the last, tangible and living connection to pre-1948 Yaffa among my family in Australia.

Aaron is actually in Palestine with me. It's once again bright and sunny, but this time we're both standing on the sands of Ajami's beach, looking the way it did before Zionist settlers invaded and ruined it with their man-made park. To our left, the beach stretches out and meets a rocky cliff in the distance. Closer to us, on our right, Yaffa's Old Town rises up on a small hill that juts out into the Mediterranean Sea.

In a small space by the medieval walls that meet the shore, we can see a huge LGBTQ progress flag being flown, with hundreds dancing and clapping along as a line of people hold hands and stomp in time with a drum beat. The dance is led by a woman dressed in a traditional thobe adorned with *tatreez*, and she waves a rainbow keffiyeh in her free hand. A queer *dabke*. The power of being able to do this in our homeland is transformative.

Aaron nudges me and jerks his head to indicate behind us. We turn around, and several meters away, where the sand becomes soil, there's a sandstone house of three stories. The home that Tata Victoria's brothers built for the whole family. My dad's beloved childhood home. On the rooftop is a *dalieh*, its lush green vine leaves providing natural shade under the blistering Mediterranean sun. Surrounding the house on three sides is an orange grove.

I see someone waving at us from underneath the *dalieh* on the roof. It's Amto. She's the only one who would recognize Aaron, after all. In this daydream, Aaron and I don't respond nor do we approach the house. My instincts tell me it's not appropriate to do so. We continue to stand there, and I imagine the waves crashing gently against our ankles as our feet sink slowly into the wet sand. The music from the nearby queer *dabke* grows louder.

On the rooftop with Amto is Ummo Ibrahim, Ummo Abdo and of course, my dad. Ummo Fouad, Ummo Basem, Amto Jamileh and Ummo Hanna—late cousins of my father whom I have met and spent considerable time with, are there too. There are several other figures on the rooftop; I'd like to think they're the elders in my grandparents' generation and other cousins of my father who have come to pass. Dad is with someone who bears a striking resemblance to him, laughing uncontrollably together over a shared joke. Siddo George. They're making up for lost time.

Tata Victoria emerges from a door with a tray of food to place on a table amid the rooftop gathering. Her favorite pastime: feeding the family. We see Amto serving a tray of fresh orange juice for her husband, her cousins, and her elders. Her signature giggle cuts through the echoing drum beats of the queer *dabke* as she reaches her brother and father in the middle of their jokes. Dad and Siddo decline the juice, but they both raise a small glass of something milky white. Arak. Everyone else, except for Amto, follows suit with their orange juice. It's as if they're all welcoming her home and this is one big family reunion. They eat and make merry, and soon everyone is clapping along with the beats of the queer *dabke*.

I imagine Aaron squeezing my hand and smiling at me. All is okay in this alternate reality. I let my mind wander to this daydream because it's what I yearn for. A space where I can bring my beloved to the land of my forebears. A family home amid the legendary orange groves of Yaffa. I like to think I am envisioning what the afterlife is like for my elders: a place where Palestine is free. A place that also includes freedom for queer Palestinians, where we can be free to be ourselves and be loved by our family.

It's just not our time, and it will not be for a while yet. The first dream in the dining room may have been rooted in sorrow in the wake of losing my father, but it marked a pivotal moment as I began my transformation into the radical, queer Palestinian I am today. The second dream, the front yard feast, was a reminder of the legacy of my Palestinian heritage. But this daydream on the shores of Ajami beach? I could well be manifesting a full circle moment. I'd like to think that it's a reminder to myself that a free Palestine will always be something worth advocating for. A just cause that will be achieved in my lifetime. A Palestine free from the occupiers, violence, and dehumanization that comes from Zionist colonization. A Palestine that honors my ancestors—and also celebrates queer joy.

We Exist

by Bint Bandora

Sisterhood Is a Lifeline
Interview with Noor, Reem, and Amal in Gaza

by Afeef Nessouli

What is hard in Gaza now is Israel's genocide and their forced starvation of everyone, queer or not. I would know, I was just in Gaza.

I am a Lebanese-American gay man, and when Zionists told me to "go to Gaza" derogatorily, I was taken aback at how little they understood the intersections of not only my identity, but the identities of my queer friends *in* Gaza. I am a reporter for The Intercept and covered the Middle East for my entire career. From March to June 2025, I went to Gaza as a volunteer health care worker with Glia International, a health care organization operating in Gaza under the World Health Organization. Three of my friends that I got to meet in person are trans women who have been suffering through Israel's genocide and, because of the monthslong blockade, are also starving. Being queer in Gaza is no cake walk, but Israel has made being Palestinian in Gaza damn near impossible. On an afternoon in mid-May, not having eaten yet, my three trans friends and I met for coffee. Here is their testimony:

"If I could travel from Gaza, I would get hair extensions and do a boob operation, but I would keep my beard," Noor explains while we sit drinking coffee at the port in Gaza City. After months of coordination with their therapist named Nancy, a Palestinian therapist and psychosocial health worker, I have been able to meet Noor, Reem, and Amal in the flesh. These three queer Palestinians living in Gaza identify as trans women. They say that it is too dangerous to present themselves as trans women in Gaza, so before the Israeli aggressions began on the Strip in 2023, they would rent private chalets at the beach on weekends together, put makeup on, dress up, and dance. "And I will do laser on my whole body, especially the bikini area and my underarms," Noor keeps explaining. "And I would cut *it* off."

Noor, Amal, and Reem have been friends since they were young and in grade school. They found each other and have been inseparable, even if that just means having secret WhatsApp group chats to talk about life and makeup. They say that there are many other trans girls in Gaza, but it is impossible to dress the way they feel in public, so they have hundreds of pictures and videos of themselves applying lipstick or in wigs on their phones. They explain that even though many men on the Strip are interested in having sex with them, like any victim of conservative men the world over, they are constantly harassed and beaten up for being feminine. They explain that many of the men they have relationships with are married to women and live secret lives. Being queer in Gaza is not acceptable, but that just means that queer people find each other online.

Noor is petite. She has brown hair and eyes and tries her damndest to coordinate the colors of every outfit. Genocide or not. She also has a really clean beard, a fresh fade, long nails, and often wears glasses. Amal is around six feet tall and has dropped to about 119 pounds. Her face is visibly gaunt, and her thighs are extremely far apart from losing so much weight. She has dark blondish hair. She belly dances and twirls every few steps out of habit, like a song is constantly playing in her head. Reem has striking blue eyes, curly brown and blond hair, and a big smile full of endearingly crooked teeth. She is the thickest of the three and says her frame can't handle the rapid weight loss.

Each girl faces violence almost every single day. "My brothers beat me up all the time and ask me why I won't work with them doing physical labor. They tell me they will kill me for being the way I am," Noor goes on. Reem jumps in to agree and talks about how her father gives her trouble all the time, but explains that if she could, "I would be just like Haifa Wehbe, the artist." Haifa Wehbe is a Lebanese singer and actress, and is considered one of the best-known artists in the Arab world. She is overtly confident and is an iconic sex symbol. Reem speaks into the microphone as the wind picks up, "I would have her exact body." The day is hot, but the area near the beach where we are sitting is so windy that no one walking by us can hear what we are talking about. Reem keeps on. "She is perfect. I want to be just like her."

Of the three, I started talking to Amal first, in 2024. I had been helping disparate humanitarian aid workers around the world get aid to Palestinians in Gaza while also helping to evacuate families and special cases through the Rafah border crossing into Cairo, Egypt. Within these groups were local Palestinian staff working alongside us. One of these people was Nancy, a certified therapist who had been offering free psychosocial care to three trans girls in Gaza. Nancy and I discussed the idea of giving them an opportunity to talk to me so that they could express their testimony. Nancy believed it would offer them some respite to explain their stories and what they were experiencing day to day as they waited to be evacuated.

While Noor, Amal, and Reem were on the list of people hoping to evacuate, the problem was that they all had to register as adult men traveling alone. Israel and Egypt are in charge of checking backgrounds of each person trying to seek asylum and being transparently outed presented too much of a risk for the girls. So, this category of evacuees—males traveling alone—historically has the hardest time getting out due to suspicions of their links to armed resistance groups like Hamas. Because of this, the girls were all rejected and are still stuck in Gaza.

The three girls have different living situations but try to see one another as often as they can get away with it. They explain that it is hard enough to operate as a feminine queer person who was assigned male at birth, but to do so with two other trans-identifying people makes it nearly impossible. "We cause a scene," Amal explains. Amal lost most of her family in the genocide and now lives alone at a school. "I don't know where they are or if they are even alive anymore" she says, as tears start streaming down her face. She says she barely eats because everything available disgusts her. I try to give her a can of tuna, but she refuses and passes it to Noor, who she says might need it more than her. As of today, when we are sitting together, aid hasn't entered the strip in about sixty days, and it shows on all of us. Reem shows me pictures of herself from before October 2023. She was quite literally double her current size. She says she fancies herself a chef. "I love to make food. I wish it was a different time so I could invite you to a proper meal." Reem lives with her father, who bullies her for being soft. She says he isolates her all of the time from going anywhere. None of the girls feel comfortable or safe in their circumstances.

Noor lives with her family, none of whom accept her sexuality or gender orientation in any way. She is regularly assaulted by her brothers for not making enough money for the family. As we sit together, she shows me pictures of herself where she is completely bruised. There are black and purple circles under her eyes from the trauma-inducing blows. Noor is vulnerable in the selfies she took, but she is also determined to document the abuse. She tells me her right jaw still hurts a lot. "We are so tired," Noor says. "It is hard to deal with bombs, and I miss chicken so much, but on top of it, we can't even be ourselves." In the middle of the conversation, Noor gets up and says, "I have to pray." She rolls out a mat in front of her, facing Mecca with the sea behind her. "Part of my identity includes being a Muslim," Noor explains before she starts. "Yes, we are Trans or queer or she-males or whatever you like to say, but we know God."

Even though things are extraordinarily difficult, given the lack of food, the acute violence from Israeli missiles strikes and quadcopters and the dangers of being outed by their community, the girls are still living as queer people. "I hooked up with a man I met on Instagram," Reem excitedly tells me. "We went to a cafe a few days ago. He took me right on the billiards table around two AM in the morning. It was beautiful really," Reem goes on. "I like them big and muscly and manly." The girls start talking frantically about their favorite things. Amal and Noor explain that they love to do makeup. "I love to dance as well, ya Afeef," Amal says, as she gets up to show off her moves. She rhythmically sucks her gut in and out and moves her hips. "I love dancing *sharqiya*" (belly dancing), she says. She sits down and shows me a video of a tall, thin belly dancer with long curly beautiful hair that touches their back in a beaded *bedlah*. As the dancer turns around, the camera locks into their face, which is covered in a beard. "This is me, this is my ideal look," Amal explains.

The three girls tell me that their dream is to all move to Cairo together. "We need to get out of here; it is too hard for girls like us," Amal explains. "The injustice of this massacre, the hunger, and also I can't even be myself." They say that if they could, they would have one store with two floors. Noor and Amal would have one floor where they sold dresses and did makeup for patrons, and Reem would have the other floor, where the patrons could have coffee and eat baked goods. As they describe their hopes and dreams, Noor breaks out in a whimper. "Oh, I am so tired, I am so tired, let this hell end," she says, slamming her fist on the table and holding tears back. She puts her head in her hands and begins to cry. The other two immediately cover her in hugs and kisses and hold her. They tell her she is beautiful and strong and not to cry. "Oh, may God show us mercy," Amal says as she holds Noor close to her.

Each of us held hands in a circle on the chairs next to the crashing waves and intensifying wind. "Please come back to the north soon," Amal pleaded. The other two joined in telling me that life was so hard but somehow my presence made it easier to deal with. "When you are here, we feel less abandoned." We decided that if we all survived this genocide, we would get a chalet together somewhere in Gaza or somewhere in Cairo or Europe for a weekend. They would do their makeup and show me their "true selves" in dresses they chose while we listened to music and hopefully ate "so much chicken." They told me that even though I wasn't a woman, I was a queen to them. Traveling to Gaza to meet them after a year of correspondence made me family to them now, which really meant we needed to make a lot more memories in the future.

For My Enemies

by Nadia Shammas

I would not deign to water your graves with my piss.
Another piece of Palestine
eternally denied you
remaining beyond your unworthy grasp.

Avoid Us Like Oxygen

by Tariq Ra'ouf

trying to avoid queerness
is like trying to avoid oxygen

you may succeed in getting away
from the type of air you don't enjoy
like the hot, thick, stickiness
of a 100% humidity day

but everywhere you go
the essence of that air
no matter the type
lingers

we linger

we are everywhere you are
and everywhere you don't want to be

the gays
the lesbians

the trans dolls
the nonbinary
everyone
and beyond

we are as essential to this earth as h2o
we thrive in all climates
and there has not been a civilization on earth
that we were not a part of

we will stand the test of time
and last longer than your religions
as we have done with the ones

that came before

just like the oxygen that fills your lungs
we are everywhere
even if you do not see us

we camouflage
like chameleons and octopi
our iridescent scales hide us
while our tentacles help us
keep hold on life

we are in your living rooms
and your restaurants
we swim in your pools
and we bathe in your sun

even when you are so sure
that we are not around...

we
see
you

you can spend all your energy
screaming about how toxic we are
or praying that we get help
telling us that god disapproves
even though we are all
part of god

fight as hard as you want
punch the air
kick it
hit us with your best shot

and you will see

it's all futile

for there is a beauty within us
that is
shimmering
undeniable
and divine

and you cannot kill divinity
or suck the oxygen out of this earth
no matter how much you want to

may god forgive you for trying

Parallel Lives

by Eman Abdelhadi

On one screen,
bulbous bones push to escape
skin translucent like the situation.
There is no formula.
I blink my eyes over those
little ashen faces.
Always, always those little ashen faces.

Helpless, I tweet.
Run from meeting to meeting,
gaze out of my second screen,
where the masses walk dogs,
sip lattes and steal glimpses into my life.

I have to focus...
    on writing the book
        that no one will read.
I spend evenings
between Xs and speech bubbles,
starting stories I don't intend to finish.
I am not the hinge,
shower me with possibility.

I'll repot the plants today.
I'll give my tears a chance to catch up with me.
I'll throw a dinner party with the damned.
I'll pick impossible recipes and brag
about having grown the herbs myself.
I'll bask in all the compliments
"You're such a good host."
"I'm just an Arab woman."

Later, I'll let you push my face into a pillow,
wrap your arms tight around my throat.
I won't tell you that I can't breathe.

I've been courting death
ever since life wouldn't text me back.
Glee when the turbulence
gets going going going.
But then I think about the other passengers
Shame can filter madness, you know?

My eyes sneak under his windshield at the intersection.
Maybe he won't look up in time.
I beckon him dare him beg him
onward onward onward
don't stop, baby keep going
please please please.
He meets my gaze while hitting the brakes.
I lament, again, that
I am simply
not

important
enough
to
warrant
a fucking
assassination.

Pati texts me to ask which of the food in the fridge she should throw out.
My rotting greens won't save anyone.
I am sorry for having all this.
I wasn't supposed to have any of this.
I don't even want any of this.
I don't care about any of this.
I'd give it all up, you know?
I would.
Really, really, I would.
Do you believe me?
I swear. I swear. I swear.
Dare me. Double dog dare me.

It was
just luck.
I got to watch them all die,
because I was the lucky one.

"Is this survivor's guilt?"
I ask another writer at her book launch.
"Guilt is selfish," she says.
So I schedule the next meeting.

Organize! Organize! Organize!
We can only win together!
Collective liberation!

Do I believe me?

I kneel down beside the curtain
and tell my therapist
I'd rather be with the dead.
He says it's uncharacteristically lazy,
scrunching his face and curling his lips
and apologizing for sounding judgmental.
"The thing is, I admire the hell out of you," he says.
"But I know you don't need that shit"

Smile for the camera.
Raise my fist for the crowd.
Shout for the mic.
I am the mother fucking revolution.
Sip a $25 martini.
It's a caviar revolution.

We didn't think it would last this long.
Is it 3ayb to start dancing again?
Go dancing at the protest
Go dancing after the protest
Go dancing as the protest

He asks me what I'm looking for
"I guess I want you to pin me against a wall
and fuck me into an abyss."
That man wasn't ready.
I smirk and release his gaze.
"You can't handle an Arab woman."

By night, I walk through Alexandria
looking for the sea.
By day, I pick through our apocalypse,
looking for somewhere to bury my grief.

Procreating in the Time of Genocide

by Hannah Moushabeck

I'm watching a tiny lifeless body flop around in her father's arms while he screams at the camera. She looks almost like a rag doll, but the sharp panic in my chest tells me the video is real.

"Hannah? The nurse is ready for you."

I walk down the long hallway of the fertility office that I have driven two hours to visit, in Albany, of all places. My local fertility clinic doesn't "in good conscience" help people of my size get pregnant. As if fat straight people don't have babies all the fucking time.

They take my height, weight, and vitals—elevated. "Don't be nervous." the nurse says, as if anything in this beige '90s Tuscan-themed office could activate me after watching a year of live-streamed genocide on my phone.

My partner and I have been talking about having a baby for years. There's a lot to consider: the cost, the environmental impact, our freedom, and the state of the world. But I have always wanted a child. My sisters like to joke that if our family were religious, our religion would be children. We worship them. This is not uncommon in Arab families. The concept of children being seen but not heard has never stained our long history. We love children as if our existence depends on it. For Palestinians, it kinda does.

The doctor finally arrives, taking in my size, and starts to talk me through the painful and expensive process of doing in vitro fertilization (IVF). In the middle of explaining the difference between a zygote and an embryo, she asks, "Is there anything causing you stress in your life right now?"

"Well, I'm Palestinian," I explain.

She blinks. "Palestine, as in, Gaza." I say.

Her face crumples in sympathy. "Oh god, it's so terrible! All those poor babies!"

I breathe, relieved that this woman, whose entire job is to bring children into the world, has an ounce of humanity and feels for the children of Gaza.

"Yeah," I say.

After being probed by an ultrasound wand she affectionately calls "Wanda," I put my clothes back on. She tells me a million things I won't remember but will Google later, and commands me to avoid the news.

On the way out she gives me a sympathetic look and leans in. "I hope they bring them home," she says.

My heart sinks, knowing full well she doesn't mean the tens of thousands of Palestinians captured and tortured by the IOF. I smile, leave the room, and request a new doctor.

My partner is a white trans masc genderqueer explosion of joy and creativity. I am half Palestinian. When we started the hunt for an eligible sperm donor, at the advice of our friends and TikTok, we decided not to buy sperm from a cryobank due to the lack of regulations and a horrifying night of watching the true crime doc *The Man with 1000 Kids.*

That left us the option of finding someone we knew. I loved this idea. Knowing the human that would help us make our kid felt reassuring. We could make sure they weren't a serial killer or worse, a sports person. And if our kiddo had questions about their genetics or history ... "Meet your spunkle, [insert cis man name]!"

The only problem with this is, as it turns out, we don't know many cis men.

The hunt began by awkwardly asking the cis men we knew in our lives. Trying to be casual and nonchalant about it. Pretending like our very future didn't depend on their answer. Our friends were enlisted to help and would text us pictures of their good-looking mailman, garbage collector, or barista, and ask, "Should we ask him?"

It wasn't till my partner was telling a story about their best friend in middle school—Chris, a sweet quiet gay boy who came out to them, after which they did in turn—that I knew we'd found the right fit. I liked the idea of having a piece of my partner's history in our kid. It seemed like the next best thing to having their DNA. We had another awkward Zoom call, and this time, he said yes! A bearded white man in his thirties with glasses and a big nose (even bigger than mine!). He was an elementary school teacher, an avid birder, and was married to a man named Adam, who ran a micro bakery out of their kitchen in Oregon. It felt like the *literal* gay dream! A few months later we were out in Oregon sampling Adam's sourdough and using a syringe to inject Chris's still-warm semen inside me and trying not to die laughing. I had forgotten about sperm. Yuck.

We tried many ways. Turkey baster IRL, IUI (a fancy, more expensive turkey baster but in the fertility office after weeks of taking intense drugs intravenously), we even tried some old Berkeley lesbian midwife trick of shipping the sperm overnight in egg yolk before shoving it up us in a sticky, smelly mess. None of these worked. Each negative pregnancy test was more disappointing than the last. It was time to graduate to the next level, which was sure to work ... IVF.

After October 7th, like every Palestinian on the planet, I was not okay. We decided to take an eight-month break from baby-making to allow me to concentrate on activism more directly without worrying about my ovulation. When it came to try again (because we're almost forty and my fertility insurance was on a timer since I quit my corporate Zionist job), I was a changed person.

Watching entire family trees get wiped off the map in 4K HD real-time while every human around me was playing catch-up—learning for the first time the fucked up seventy-six-year history of the extermination of my people and asking naive questions—changes a person. Staying awake beside the phone when you've lost contact with your friends in Gaza, while Al Jazeera plays nothing but a live video stream of a dark city occasionally lit up with the flashes of air strikes, and wondering if your friends are slowly suffocating to death under rubble—changes you. Watching every "woke" liberal friend who proudly displayed their BLM signs and "did the work" after June 2020 awkwardly turn away and ignore your pleas while still wearing their "Resist" T-shirts— changes you.

My access to top medical services and care disgust me while I watch the reports of women in Gaza giving birth in tents and have C-sections without anesthetic. I follow as the hospitals are bombed and babies are made to share incubators, only to be left to die when IOF soldiers occupy the building.

I turn to the writings of poets and storytellers who promise a time when it will be over. I repost memes about Palestinians as seeds and being buried, only to rise again. How the grandchildren of Nakba survivors will never forget and one day return. I feel the weight of my ancestors on my shoulders as I change every part of my life in service of the cause. I quit my job. I fundraise. I organize.

Somehow, the ethnic cleansing of my people is tangled up in my efforts to get pregnant, like my womb alone can erase the horrors of the past. That bringing more Palestinian babies into this world is part of my resistance to the violent erasure of my people. *God, now I sound like a fucking trad wife.*

When it comes to doing IVF, there are complications. It requires surgery. And another. Luckily, we have two uteruses to play with, so my partner and I both extract eggs. And the discussion begins.

Whose eggs do we use? *It doesn't matter, right?* We just want a healthy baby, genetics be damned ... right? Suddenly, the idea of half of me, my genetics, my ancestry, the hard-fought, tooth-and-nail part of me that was always too controversial, too loud, too difficult, existed too much, would not be continued in my lineage. My family would be majority European white, and the part of me that has struggled to not drown out my Arab self in a suffocating white supremacist country would lose. I would be an anomaly in my white majority household.

"They will *still* be Palestinian, because you are!" friends reassured me. I can't help but think of the photographs of middle-class white women in their pink pussy hats determinedly holding signs saying, "We are ALL Palestinian."

But they won't be Palestinian. I know the overwhelming pull of white supremacy. I know how it has served me. My white skin making me cute and approachable, employable and friendly, safe and nonthreatening. I know the intoxication of putting "British" in your Tinder profile only to receive triple the matches than before. It won't be their fault. It's just math. Being white in America will give them a better life.

A mix-up at the lab means that when it comes time to make my eggs into embryos, we have run out of sweet gay birder sperm. We have twenty-four hours to find some more or my eggs may not fertilize.

Every hurdle that we have overcome, every dime to get here, only to be waylaid again! I am so angry. My brain shouts, "*Are Zionists trying to stop me from making Palestinian babies?*" I imagine one of the Zionist Karens who write posts about me as a "Hamas-sympathizer" and "antisemite" sneaking into the fertility lab in the middle of the night. I imagine her leaning over our little vials and whispering, "There's no such thing as Palestine" before she tips over the rack and laughs as she hears them shatter on the floor.

Did I mention that hormones make me paranoid?

So, I do what any millennial would do. I Google "Buy sperm. Rush order." Now, before we decided to go with a known donor, I used to look at cryobank sites all the time. It's fun. It has all the same joys of swiping on Tinder or browsing on Zillow, wondering what could be. Never once in the many months of swiping did I find a Palestinian donor. The very few Middle Eastern donors I did find were Israeli, and the idea of having colonizer sperm inside me turned me off the entire category. What does Middle Eastern mean anyway? Middle and East of where? *EXACTLY.*

This time, when I opened the site, a new donor alert pops up. Donor nickname: Proud Palestinian. *Holy shit.* He was perfect. He loves Palestinian food and music. He's dedicated to his family and culture. He plays the oud. And he's a Christian Palestinian, no less! Plus... he's in medical school. I could feel my Tata's approval from beyond the grave. "He's from a very good family."

Hot tip for Arab queers in the future: If you're a queer uterus-haver, you don't need to marry the perfect Arab man; just be gay and use their sperm! Everyone wins.

After sharing his photos and description with my family everyone seemed positively giddy, but there was one question looming: What if we are related? It's not a crazy question. Palestinians in the diaspora all seem to know one another, and we all originate from a very small piece of land, so the odds are not in my favor. I am not exaggerating. For example, when coediting this book with George Abraham, we found out that we are cousins! (Good thing I didn't ask them for sperm. lolz.)

After my *khalto*'s very scientific investigation, she determines that because of the white suit that my donor was wearing in one photo, he was likely Catholic and we are Greek Orthodox, so if we were related, it was only through marriage. Plus, according to my aunt, "He has a Lebanese chin!" Feeling some relief, we decided to just go for it. (Don't worry, we did a DNA test too, just to be sure.)

The sperm was ordered and delivered, just in time to meet my eggs and do a little anti-Zionist fertility *dabke* in a petri dish and voilà!, four healthy zygotes (not yet embryos).

Our child would not only carry the DNA of my Nakba-surviving grandparents, but my lineage would not dilute; it would become *more* Palestinian.

As the genocide worsened, so did my health, with a diagnosis of long Covid taking me out of the baby-making game. Luckily, my team has multiple players and my partner decided to step up to the plate. On one perfect day of thrifting, donut eating, and a drive to the fertility clinic, I held their hand and cheered them on as we watched our little zygote shoot from the catheter into their uterus. Bull's-eye.

Just a little fleck in the night' sky. We decided to (temporarily) call her Bella Fleck after the bearded banjo player. Bella, our little but fierce, genetically engineered but resilient cluster of cells was so determined to be in the world that she toppled her way joyfully out of the catheter, before zinging around the uterus and promptly bouncing her way up a fallopian tube.

Ectopic. *Shit.*

After positive pregnancy tests lined our baby altar, we told people too soon, only to have to painfully update them a few weeks later. Bella turned from our hopeful spark of a future to a shard of glass that could kill the one I loved before my very eyes.

We were two hours from home, in the Tuscan-beige clinic room, when we were told that my sweet, round, ready-to-be-Baba partner had to have it removed or they could die. My mind can't stop the carousel of images of dead babies that I have held in my hand for the past two years, and swipe and swipe and swipe.

While slow but calm tears slipped down their bearded cheeks, my brain short-circuited. In Trump's America, my PREGNANT TRANS partner, carrying our PALESTINIAN zygote, needed an ABORTION or they would die. Call FOX News. I was sure my nemesis, Zionist Karen, was going to pop out from around the wrought iron candelabra and dance a little jig to the tune of "Ding, Dong! The Witch Is Dead." My rage blooms.

The doctors were lovely, and all expressed sympathy for our loss. Thank god for living in a state where the operation was smooth and comfortable and covered (mostly) by insurance. My partner took my breath away. Such bravery. Such strength. They said goodbye to their fallopian tubes and asked to hear the zygote's heartbeat. I washed the iodine off their body after surgery so they looked less like an Oompa-Loompa and marveled at our privilege.

While I sit in the recovery room, waiting for my partner to wake from their post-surgery slumber, my phone is blowing up. A Zionist Karen has testified in the Massachusetts Special Commission on Combatting Antisemitism, another charade of governance by Zionists trying to conflate antisemitism with anything opposing the genocidal actions of an apartheid state. In her testimony, she named *my visit to a local school* as evidence of antisemitism. Today it appeared on the front page of my local newspaper. A newspaper I aspired to one day be in as a child.

Now, sitting in the hospital with my sweet partner, I wonder what world we are bringing a child into. Is it selfish of me to want my child to be Palestinian? Can I protect them from all this? These thoughts are on my mind as I bring my resilient, healing partner home.

Grief and loss are no strangers in our house.

I place the loss on the pile and move forward. My survivor's guilt tells me, *"Who am I to have a child? Why me, when so many children have been taken?*" My therapist asks me, "Who does this guilt serve?"

Yesterday, I threw away the positive pregnancy tests that were collecting dust on our baby altar. I am preparing my body to try again. I have scraps of hope and energy that I collect and throw together and hope it will be enough.

But my heart is broken: for Gaza, for Bella, for my family, for my community. Rage burns slowly and consistently inside me.

They say to be calm and stress-free when you are trying to get pregnant. Now, when the nurse asks, "Is there anything stressful in your life?" I just laugh.

Own Dawn

by Maria

I speak to you of temporalities
as if I ever witnessed a dawn
that I could ever call my own

this world has ended
a thousand times for us
and will end a thousand more

we learned the choreography of farewell
like we learned the voices of our own mothers
with our own body on our own soil

with our own blood on our own soil
borders have been drawn
and we chose to remember
but we did not choose
the rhythm
the distance
the curves of the Carmel
the flow of the Yarmouk

and I have nothing to hide
nothing to hide
and nothing to discover
but my own mortality

here is my bed
here is the coastline
here are the gates of Jerusalem
here is the wheat of the Galilee
here is my sorrow
my sweat
my adam's apple
here is a world
that has ended many times before

so I will kiss the leftovers of sleep from your face
you will heat the water
I will make the bed
for the world might
or might not
begin again today.

Suture Fragmentations—A Note on Return

by Sarona Abuaker

"To stand with us in this circle with its center everywhere and its circumference now/here is to be under a spell. A pleasure to meet you here: enchanted"[2]

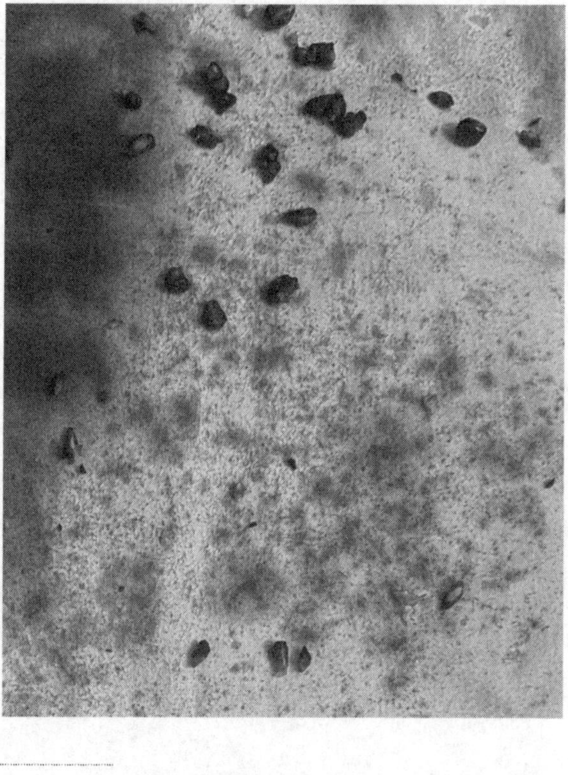

2 Shin, S. and Tamás, R. *SPELLS: 21st Century Occult Poetry*. Ignota Books (2018).

Shortly after finishing an essay exploring how Palestinians' abilities to produce aesthetics inherently carves new spaces to resist Israeli settler colonialism, I visited Basma Alsharif's exhibition "The Gap Between Us" at the Mosaic Rooms in London.[3] It was Alsharif's first independent UK exhibition, comprised of three pieces originating from different moments in her practice. Overlaying a multiplicity of images and sounds from original film footage taken from different locations she visited, Alsharif stitches together rich tapestries of reimagined spaces and times as an intimate navigation through her ideas of what Palestinian imagination and memory re/building can look like as a Palestinian in diaspora. Filming in France, Italy, California, the Gaza Strip, Malta, and Athens, she weaves aesthetics familiar to the Palestinian national struggle amongst a backdrop of unfamiliar landscapes, and interrogates the elasticity of what is constituted as familiar Palestinian cultural forms by challenging the audience and herself with the question, "What do you do when civilization has failed you? What happens if the Right of Return is never granted—what will this mean for Palestinians?"[4]

3 Alsharif, B. The Gap Between Us. (Film Footage) London: The Mosaic Rooms (2018).

4 Basma Alsharif by Aily Nash. 2015. BOMB. Available at: bombmagazine.org/articles/basma-alsharif/

To be oriented around something is not so much to take up that thing, as to be taken up by something, such that one might even become what it is that is ‘around’[5]”

5 Ahmed, S. 2006. *Queer Phenomenology: Orientations, Objects, Others*. Duke University Press (2006).

Moving from piece to piece, Alsharif's unflinching questions on return, memory re/building, and futuristic aesthetic reconfigurations have followed and not left me since. Emerging from the collision of her cultural forms constituting as Palestinian expressions was not only a reshaped understanding of resistance, but a shift in how to engage with and produce Palestine and Palestinians' relationship with diaspora. The conditions involved in experiencing displacement, nation-state building, and identity formation are not unique to Palestinians or to the Palestinian national struggle. These themes, however, have become synonymous to Palestinian ontology due to their repetition and juxtaposition within Palestinian cultural production as strategic methods to evoke indigenous claims in the face of ongoing Israeli settler colonialism.

Necessitating the physical and cultural erasure of the indigenous settler colonialism "comes with the intention of making a new home on the land, a homemaking that insists on settler sovereignty over all things in their new domain."[6] The reality of dispossession impacts Palestinians' ways of engaging, moving in, and experiencing Palestine on the physical realm of being able to access the land. This physical uprooting, and the response to it, is a production of Palestinian-ness tied to a "place-bound definition (which) focuses on return, and home is defined as from where one came."[7] Returning to Palestine functions as not only the point of origin for how Palestinians come to identify them-

6 Tuck, E. and Yang, K. "Decolonization Is Not a Metaphor." *Decolonization: Indigeneity, Education & Society*, 1(1), 2012, pp.1–40. jps.library.utoronto.ca/index.php/des/article/view/18630.

7 Peteet, J. "Problematizing a Palestinian Diaspora." *International Journal of Middle East Studies*, 39(04), 2007, pp.1–21.

selves, but as an activator for aesthetic production as it reflects conditions of exile. Expressions of return in all its dimensions have become the prevailing cultural discourse for engagement with Palestine and Palestinian-ness, especially for Palestinians in diaspora. When Palestinians' common capacity to engage with themselves exists mainly through this framework, how does this shape Palestinian diasporic ontologies? What happens when this concept of return is no longer the exclusive departure point?

⋆

Return
"to come back or
go back to a place or
person/architecturally—
continue (a wall) in a changed
direction, especially at
right angles[8]

The notion of return, or returning, glimmers
r i p p l i n g m o v e m e n t s.

This is a poem colonizers
will
cut
their hands on
chronic wounds
splintering

8 Definition of "return." Merriam-Webster.com

Return is inherently an experiment in phenomenology; to go or come back is a beckoning of how to arrive. Alsharif's gaps directs the viewer to stitched spatialities and temporalities in order to interrogate return. It is here, in this moment of being re-turned to experience a return by her films I found what was relegated to the background of my life but I was
always– – – – x

x – – – – – – a r r i v i n g t o – – – – – – – x

Palestinian-ness as a queer dimension and the possibilities of queering return– – – x

*

Arriving
involves questions
timing, space, direction.
Can we arrive, recognize we are arriving
if it is not thought out? It is a question of being in
a certain order—one that defies settler-colonial ordering.
To arrive to a place not on the map means thinking beyond
what we see
pushing my body and vision in different, multiple ways to
create new shapes, forms of thought.

We keep moving
I hear her
he didn't
fast

throw the

he walks
taking off

say
roll down his window
enough to

Molotov.
                    Re/(O)pen
from Lebanon to Syria
his socks
he finds
      his skin comes off.

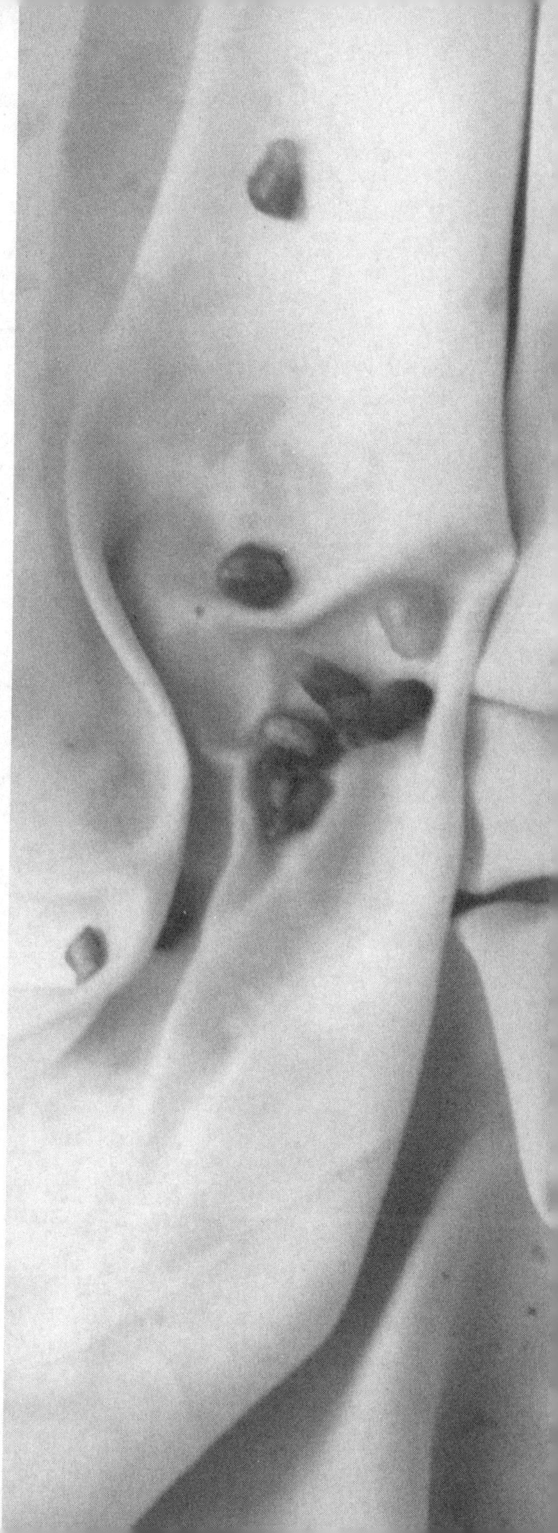

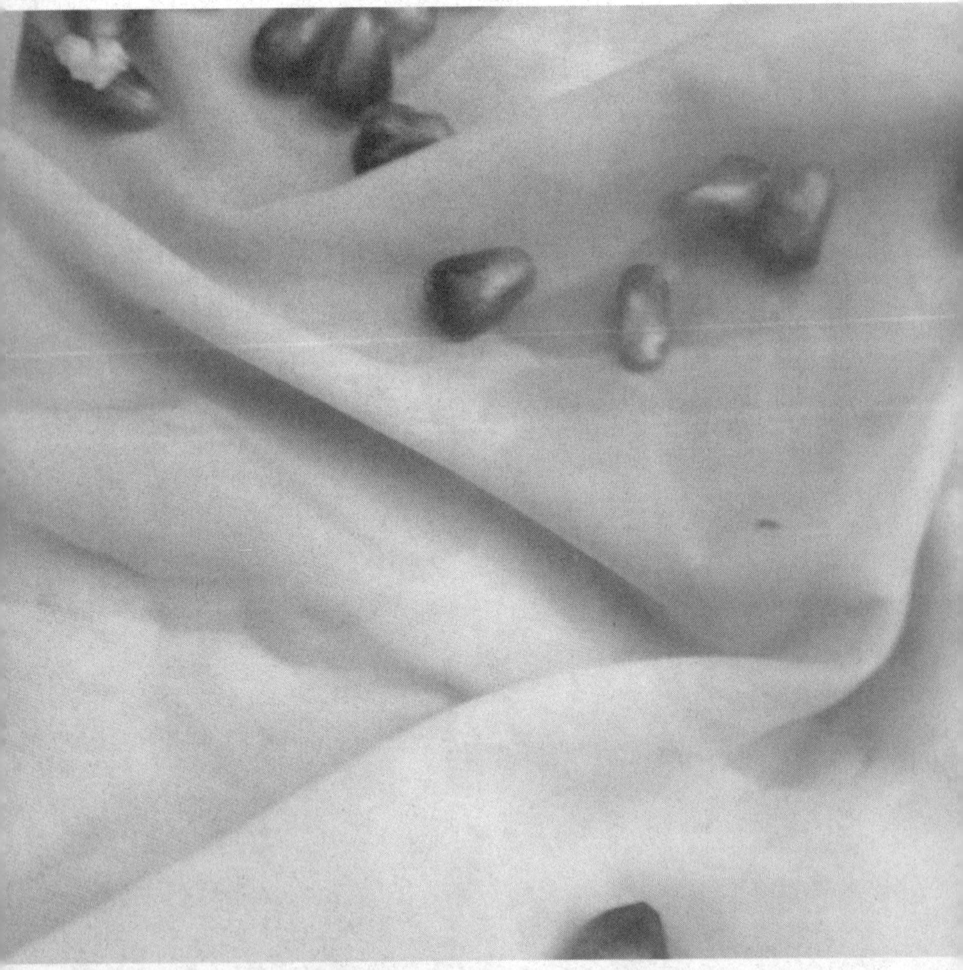

"Becoming reoriented
which involves the disorientation of encountering
the world differently, made me wonder about orientation
and how much 'feeling at home'
or knowing which way we are facing
is about the making of worlds"[9]

9 Ahmed 2006

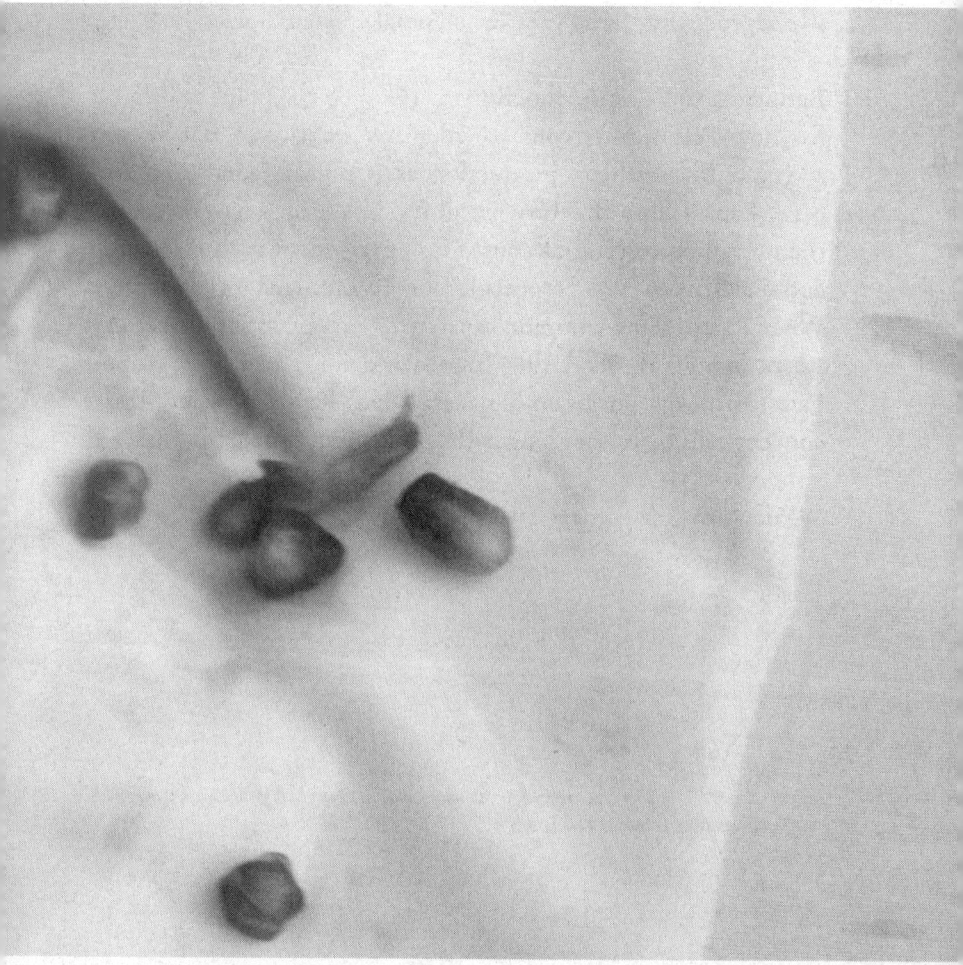

Alsharif's pieces spoke to a queerness already present; I was able to recognize the beats, rhythms, sutured landscapes, and disorientations for they mirrored, resonated with my own. Queerness of/being out of place in (diaspora), whilst pointing to queerness in Palestinian-ness. Her films made me think of how my experience of inheriting a homeland with a certain direction towards it, with a certain nature of relationality; to be Palestinian in many ways is to be constituted as an "unnatural"[10] occurrence for it pushes back against a hegemonic narrative reproducing Israel's settler-colonial epistemologies.

Returning to Palestine functions as not only the point of origin for how Palestinians come to identify themselves, but as an activator for aesthetic production as it reflects conditions of exile. Expressions of return in all its dimensions have become the prevailing cultural discourse for engagement with Palestine and Palestinian-ness, especially for Palestinians in diaspora. When Palestinians' common capacity to engage with themselves exists mainly through this framework, how does this shape Palestinian diasporic ontologies? What happens when this concept of return is no longer the exclusive departure point?

We don't scatter
we are
elastic
stretching

10 Seymour, N. *Strange Natures: Futurity, Empathy, and the Queer Ecological Imagination.* University of Illinois Press (2013)

Without our ancestor's
masks (what are they?)

beyond
their wildest dreams

Queerness here means the processes and acts of re-orienting return in relation to times, spaces, us. Return has always, then, been conceived as "unnatural," for it is a practice of making an order beyond the state-sanctioned order which we live today of "capitalist domestication"[11] and settler-colonial regimes. I propose return as practice, queering return so it realigns with orientations of possibility, a way of directing through future-thinking. Return as spatial occurrences.

11 Ibid.

How does queer phenomenology help us think about living return in different spaces and being re-turned in spaces? It is an inching "towards," and I want to think about what moving a towards and where that towards may be, to retexturize the feel of life

we shape ourselves
with the force
of each other
carve new spaces and times
wringing out
sea water

I am moved to queer return as a possibility of occurring and being encountered in many places for I am moved by it in a multiplicity of spaces, times, touches, gestures and articulations. This piece is an attempt to start re-directing, gathering my bearings and senses, only to return to them back to you as a reader and see what takes shape in this exchange. Creating new forms means moving, taking other directions and making new movements. There are specificities to how return gathers itself around me, and my intention is to highlight who is able to face return. There are tensions in the particularities of facing return one way for it is not one dimension or position. This is also an experiment in relationalities.

I am arriving in return/its multiplicity of dimensions.

* * *

Categorizing strictly through the nation-state has become an atmospheric experience developing and shaping our senses of the world, for it lends itself as an inherent departure point for how people imagine themselves, and has become the only legitimate way of conceptualizing oneself. Legitimate here means the way in which hegemonic structural systems come to envelop one's aura through their recognizability of nation-ness and belonging to a state. Being Palestinian in many ways is queer due to the multiple dimensions I occupy—past, present, future, to not be recognized by states, inheriting a homeland without being in it. I am embodying an encapsulation of times, spaces, legacies and fragments. These fragmentations are a result of the establishment of Israel in 1948 "resulting in the devastation of Palestinian society. At least 80 percent of the Palestinians who lived in the major part of Palestine upon which Israel was established—more than 77 percent of Palestine's territory—became refugees."[12] The Nakba—the catastrophe—simultaneously induced an uprooting in common Palestinian senses and expression. It is for this reason that I use fragmentation as a form for writing this piece.

the children
of those who were expelled
were colors.
Each one imbued
turning to each other and say
what if we were there
at the same time
together

12 Abu-Lughod, L. and Sa'di, A. *Nakba: Palestine, 1948, and the Claims of Memory*. Columbia University Press, 2007, pp.1–24.

Settler-colonialism ruptures the
cultivated by the indigenous to
spaces splinter and become
from oral narrativization to
time and spaces which were
in forms, textures, gestures—it is experiencing shock and
level

forms of times and spaces
the land; these times and spaces
carried in different ways,
cultural production. The
violently uprooted change
tongue, memory and touch
disorientation on every

The creation and maintenance of Israel relies on the erasure of
sensory experiences and understandings constituting
Palestinian-ness. Erasure of sensory experiences, being able to
locate oneself

            occurs

                        on

            multiple

(sometimes dehiscent
i |close| the stitches
find them re/(o)pened
tissue replaces
dermis as epidermis in motion
biochemical immunity)

levels

* * *

Settler-colonial erasure involves the unbinding of lines drawn around and on the surfaces, which come to be felt as fact and knowledge: a violent systematic deliberate targeting to unravel what gives form to our lives. From redrawing lines on a map, constituting written, textual forms as more "valid" than oral forms narrativizing experiences, freezing Palestinian bank accounts, stealing literature, films and images, to home demolitions and expulsions, Israeli settler-colonialism, like other examples of settler-colonialism, embodies how colonial state-building practices relies on the literal and aesthetic reorientating of the indigenous.

Taking the "desert to make it bloom," a common trope emerging from Israeli settler colonial Soviet style posters,[13] showing from a bird's-eye-view a lush valley sunken by the weight of happy, well-fed and cultivated trees meant to be representing Jaffa. Each tree bright, carrying engorged ripe sun-blasted oranges with a hand reaching towards the orange, a hand outstretched ready and eager to pick the fruity gem the land produced, for the land is grateful that a civilizing force has swept over it. The force is often embodied through the figure represented as a woman, smiling coyly as she picks the oranges for it is not only produce she is gathering, she is also producing lines of power and being received in certain directions solidifying the making of Israel.

13 Sivan, E. "Jaffa, the Orange's Clockwork." Video (2009).

As said woman picks oranges, lines appear on the land where homes once were – – – – straightening lines, where native homes embody the "perversion," the "queerness," the "odd" ways in which the native inhabits the space. The being of Palestinianness in a space transformed into a threat to the state-building order; to be Palestinian embodied a direction of not just "backwards" but of being bent towards an idea, a physical discomfort for the new state because it was and continues to be a body that takes up space and in taking up space produces a shape which is not desired.

"The contemporary history of the Palestinians turns on a key date: 1948. That year, a country and its people disappeared from maps and dictionaries . . . 'The Palestinian people does not exist,' and henceforth the Palestinians would be referred to by general, conveniently vague terms, as either 'refugees,' or in the case of a small minority that had managed to escape the generalized expulsion, 'Israeli Arabs.' A long absence was beginning"[14]

14 Abu-Lughod and Sa'di 2007.

Palestinian-ness became a being that was outside of state logic. And as this line of thinking follows, we emanate a queerness for "when bodies 'arrive' that don't extend the lines already extended by spaces, then those spaces might even appear 'slantwise' or 'oblique.'"[15]

The length of time maintaining expulsions, and how dominance is reasserted through the settler-colonial apparatus, whether here or there, accumulate and matter. Forms of dominance by Israel are expressed through the ability to create distances. Return is mainly approached as a thing which must appear only because it is perceived as a moment that has been blocked from its entry. Distance is not only a physical separation. Distances are not composed of matters which end when the separation ends, or when a recognized form of arrival arrives. It takes work to illuminate and thrive amidst gaps and spaces—but what about the matters at hand which we re-turn to do the work of return(ing) towards these openings and fragments? If return(ing) will take on the shapes of the conditioning from our bodies, who will be the ones who shape our pasts/presents/futures? The Nakba did not end; it only continues to devastate in refashioned ways.

15 Ahmed 2006.

It is here I intervene in a form of return. I want to turn now to look at the matter return can be/is made of. This attempt of thinking through return is an invitation to think about what matters about ourselves. The stuff of situating, measuring, arriving, leaving to and in around/ourselves.

Suture Fragmentations—A Note on Return *by Sarona Abuaker*

Return is an embodiment of labor and work—who is taking it upon themselves to ensure return emerging? Writing this piece is a form of labor. I am suggesting return(ing) can be/is composed of such matters, such labors at hand. There is a question of the value of looking at how these navigations matter at all, especially to return(s). The value of tensions, unfurling them, matter for behavior matters. Return(ing) is not a matter at hand that should be brushed off, taken into others hands who will bring forth return (ing) as a commodity, which, presented by hegemonic powers, "is changed into something transcendent."[16]

Walking through Ramallah in spring 2019 underneath construction and buildings, increasing in height by the year, positioning visions of Prada and Dolce & Gabbana conveniently located underneath luxury flats. Futures front and center to pedestrians while the leadership keeps billboards than the people or streets themselves. These are affects brought forth from the non-queerness of this world.

Couture shops able to exist more easily than the very people
who've been here for centuries.
wanting)

A disorienting touch, senses of fugitivity. I am gripped (in
to not be right
side
          up
   if this vision is what is meant
to be
the linear perceptible path.

16 Ibid.

* * *

Neoliberal imaginations taking up space, the effects of histories co-opted for state-building as a practice for a return exclusively enjoyed by banks, private investors, newly gated community owners. A commodification of practices shape the form of return—is "it" still return if the very motions that kicked my mother, sister and I out of our home in the states take space in Palestine under a different flag?

Return(ing) is not about trying to find forgiveness/refuge from debt in one boundary only to accumulate it in another. Return(ing) is not about showing solidarity for blackness in one place/language only to arrive to another and allow those very poisoning anti-black articulations/gestures to proliferate in a different tongue.

Return is not something separate from our contact with
others; it is a shape made
by

our

relationalities

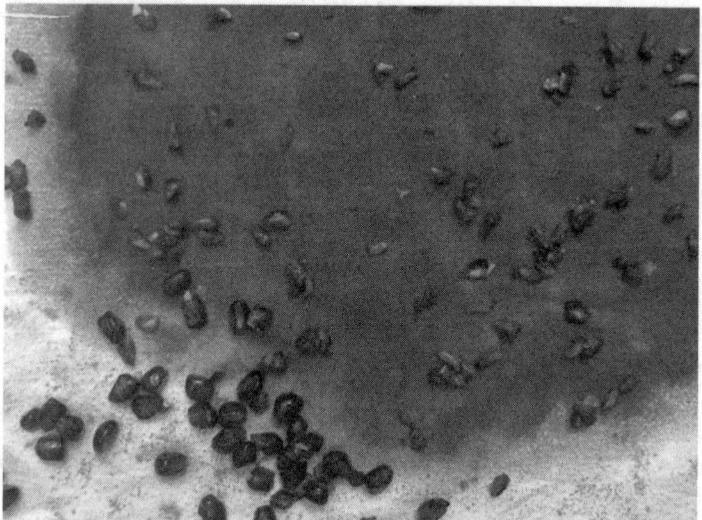

Where am I? Why is this here? What is here and what needs to be in its place?
It is a "queer disorientation, the absence of coherence, but not of things, in the moving presence of absolutely nothing."[17]
It is a hold unlike any other.

Soldiers fire tear gas
i ran holding myself to the sea
washing away the agent only to find our photographs

drowned

17 Harney, S. and Moten, F. *The Undercommons: Fugitive Planning & Black Study*. Wivenhoe: Minor Compositions (2013)

Understandings of return often arrive at forms of touch/I have a dimension of return for it is a right/which I am enshrined with by *having* UN Resolution 194.

The United Nations General Assembly adopts resolution 194 (III), resolving that "refugees wishing to return to their homes and live at peace with their neighbours should be permitted to do so at the earliest practicable date, and that compensation should be paid for the property of those choosing not to return and for loss of or damage to property which, under principles of international law or equity, should be made good by the Governments or authorities responsible."."[18]

As the UN General Assembly described in the above paragraph in 1948, the emergence of return in this proscribed space and time relies on certain positionalities, certain directions to be taken place. Return must be "practicable," the qualities of this practicable return must be made "good" (for whom?) or compensated (by whose measure?) by the "Governments or authorities responsible" (when has this ever happened?).

Under whose return is this practicable? Nonetheless, "refugees" is left completely unformed—one dimensional. Static. Return emerges as a stack of bones in the corner. Swept aside. Out of sight out of mind. Where is return in any "peace process" resolution, other than the nuisance it presents itself to be—the insect on the ground of your kitchen floor scuttling away with the corner of your favorite independence day cake in its mouth.

18 UN General Assembly 194 UNRWA www.unrwa.org/content/resolution-194

What position does this interpretation, this practice, this linear, straight state suit making return leave us in? This isn't to dismiss the dire necessity of this dimension of return needing to happen; a physical return especially for those who are experiencing forms of limbo for the last several decades. I know all too well the number of spaces my blue U.S.A. passport allows me to breezily walk into—entering the United Kingdom where I currently reside the borders become more insidiously porous through technological aesthetic data harvesting methods. No more do I oftentimes need a person to ask me where I was—I hold a document enshrined with a status which allows me to head straight to machines where I swipe it. Doors open and I walk into a different country. Buying fruits at the self-checkout in Sainsbury's can often feel more like a tedious task than the border. This does not mean I am not in the direct line of violence—it means the line I am "walking into in that moment, in that space, is extended to me in this particular dimension."[19]

19 Ahmed 2006.

Are these the forces we leave to shape return? Britain after all has a role in this mess.

I am set in a different direction quite literally from others who hold other documents from other places. And the state sanctifies itself to hold these people differently ---------- --------
----------------x------------------->
----x-------------------x-----------------x
x-----------------T h e l i n e
designed to walk within is quite literally straight whereas people who hold "other" documents require more spaces—

to wait

to stand

more cubicles to show the line is

not to be followed without a break but to expect breaks

to expect deviations for you/your (body) becomes the deviation. You become questioned, you become the question in and of itself which must be answered—the first curiosity always aligning with that of spatiality

"where have you come from?"

In many ways I hold two molecular embodiments—benefiting from being born in a space which institutionally rejects my very embodiment if I were to be born in the city where my mother was born.

(if someone is denied access to Jerusalem for over 40 years because they are constituted as a threat based solely on their nationality, denied a return, to then be granted a visa after reaching the age of 50 for the state no longer considers this numerical arrival a threat—is this deviance restored to a rightful state order? Their being, at one point constituted as a perversion to the state's ethno-sanctity, now granted permission to be in these certain spatialities—new lines open, new orientations are available, but the texture is still that of the states, of the settler-colonial ordering.)

"And so it is we remain in the hold, in the break, as if entering again and again the broken world, to trace the visionary company and join it."

We deviate in our world-making. I remain in this hold—crashing and crashing into this world, shattering and re-shattering to see the fragments and find ways of making new worlds in these profound and heart-wrenching futurisms. "Tracing" as Moten and Stefanno say, the line of deviations, return to spaces we've been only to find ourselves re-turned. Orienting to others in these visionary lines. I take certain directions to make certain returns—to make those returns/desires seem possible. I align with other's lines if their return(ings)

is a matter of being. Being in return, being returned, be-coming return. It is "the refugee" who needs to be "returned"—a certain position, a deviation from state-making order. Taking it upon ourselves of doing the work to ensure return does not become a commodity.

To own what I am made of/making and what I aim to be, to push forward return as not a single act dictated by hegemonic states, but as pieces of practices encompassing every dimension of life means return is an emancipation of the senses; I push return forward not as a policy which must wait until a linear achievement of Palestinian sovereignty becomes a land form. It is not the end point—it is an ongoing departure. Queering return by repositioning it as not only a physical dimension of physically returning to Palestine if that is what is chosen by Palestinians, but also occupying multiple times and spaces of practice for Palestinian-ness occupies those very things. I am queering return by facing it as a Palestinian born and raised outside of Palestine—there is a plurality of things within Palestinian-ness which are relegated to the background by hegemonic powers; the starkest example is recognizability of Palestine/Palestinians, including return and also the role of diaspora in world-making.

Fugitivity
is
a rhythm
soft
in the under
salve palliates
the proliferations
we do not need to be
assuaged
we need to set fire

x – – – – –   – – – – – x

love lessons across the space/time continuum

by Mejdulene Bernard Shomali

Illinois 1982

My mother cried when she had me, her fourth child, another girl. She'd been told by the doctors that I was a boy. I don't know how I came to know this story, except to say my parents' expectations for my sisters and me were always very high and very clear. And that my birth, however loved I was in my family, was a disappointment. I like to joke that this moment is my queer root, a little throwback to homosexuality as a symptom of gender inversion, but realistically, I don't believe in queer roots and am too happily femme. Sometimes, I think my comfort in femininity is one of the reasons I did not come to my queerness sooner. I didn't read to myself as deviating from any norms, except in my fatness.

To grow up in a highly feminine household meant a keen and early awareness of how to do gender. My mother and sisters would spend hours getting ready in the morning—working out, doing their hair and makeup, finding the right clothes. It seemed like my father rolled out of bed and went to work with one stop in the bathroom for basic cleanliness. Before returning to

Palestine, my four siblings and I lived in a two-bedroom apartment with one bathroom. The queue for the bathroom was long and we had to stagger our timing to make it work. For parties and events, my sisters would style my hair into big '80s blowouts. At the mall, my mother would find one or two dresses that fit girls my size. At school we wore uniforms, and we had to order the biggest option in the Sears catalog. My fatness was family discourse. What I ate, how much of it. How I dressed, how I couldn't dress. Diets and "fasts" and programs. Everything I understood about my body I understood first through its fatness.

I wasn't always fat. In both my memory and visual record, my body started to get bigger than other kids my age around eight. It just happened. I couldn't understand at the time, how or why or what had shifted, except that suddenly my body was wrong and needed to be fixed. It wasn't until I was in my late twenties that I realized the shift in my body's size and comportment coincided with my first experiences of sexual abuse. There are a handful of studies about this correlation. They range in their reasoning, but the general idea is that the trauma of sexual abuse might produce habits or physiological systemic responses that cause weight gain and/or prevent weight loss. I don't know what to do with this information exactly, especially because I no longer want or need to excuse or explain my fatness. This body, holding fast against, against.

Michigan 1987
I cried on the second day of kindergarten because I forgot my name tag at home. On the last day, my kindergarten teacher wanted to hold me back, too young as an October baby. Instead, my parents had my older sisters tutor me all summer. I wore

glasses and my headband was always falling into my face. My parents drove a station wagon the other kids called the Shomali yacht. In the second grade, I was put into a slow readers' group. In the third grade, I got detention for refusing to leave the bathroom after a fight with one of my girl friends. A boy pinched my butt in class and got away with it. I had a booming voice for doing the readings in church. In the fourth grade, my teacher said I didn't pay for a yearbook but I knew I did, and I was too upset and embarrassed to ask my parents for more money to get one. I knew we were poor; we got free lunches and subsidized tuition. My mother once brough maklouba to a school potluck and only one person from my class liked it. That soft boy became my crush for the next few years. I was too big, I didn't play sports, I couldn't go to sleepovers, I didn't seem to be good at anything. I wore oversized T-shirts and couldn't figure out where my family ended and I began. Once during a fundraiser for the Flint chapter of the Beit Sahour association, two girls who I thought were my friends locked me into the bathroom and turned off the lights when they learned I weighed 100 pounds. At some point, *The Little Mermaid* came out, and we'd laugh and pretend Baba was King Triton advising us Arabs/merpeople against American boys/humans.

Beit Sahour 1993

D was my cousin, several times removed. I met her at family functions the summer I arrived in Palestine, and we became friends. By the end of my first year there, we were best friends, so much so that I asked my father to transfer me from the American school in Jerusalem to the Arabic school in Beit Sahour. We had the intensity of friendship between young girls that felt all encompassing. We adopted one another's speech patterns; we came up with songs together; we shared secrets. I hadn't wanted to move, of course. What ten-year-old wants to change schools, let alone countries? Palestine was a shock to the system, but she softened it. She taught me what to wear, how to speak to boys, whom to befriend. She taught me how to be a girl, there.

It will come as no surprise that D was beautiful. She had rich brown hair, tight with curls against burnt umber skin. Her eyes were wide and long-lashed, her nose straight with a sculpted tip and full lips that predated the use of Instagram filters or filler, but appeared as perfectly as though they were used. She had a fragility I lacked—perhaps her small size in comparison to my large body. It always felt to me like girls in Palestine weren't fat. While we were never compared to one another directly, my excess was another aspect of what I lacked. I think it is tempting for queer people who come out later in life to revisit their childhoods and remark on the intensity of their friendships, the kind of queer underpinning our intimacy might suggest. I know I have done it myself. But when I think about our friendship, I don't register the depth as romantic or sexual. Despite my strangeness, D saw me and accepted me. I felt chosen by her, the most popular girl in our class. And I did not become her fat friend, a side character. I became popular too. Of all the transformations I have made in my life, the shift from bottle-bottom glasses weirdo to smiling, smizing tween has been the most unlikely. Of course I loved her; of course she was my intimate friend. But she was not a crush or an unrequited love. She loved me the same way, and it was through her that I came to love my life in Palestine.

Michigan 1997

When I left Beit Sahour, something broke in me that cannot be repaired. Returning to the US was the trigger on a lifetime of melancholy, major depression, and suicidal ideation. D and I spoke on the phone and wrote one another letters, but the absence of physical togetherness gave way to other kinds of distance. Two years after we moved back to the US, we visited Palestine. Life had moved on in Beit Sahour without me; another new girl had joined my class and became beloved. Couples broke up and reformed. What had been simmering under the surface, the sexual awakening that had been building in adolescence, was now bubbling. That summer I spent a lot of time with D, but I recall clearly the difference in our goodbyes. The realization that the Palestine I loved could live without me and I had better learn to live without it.

Back in the US I had become still; I had become smaller in spirit and larger in size. The first years back are a blur in my memory, something hazy and painful. I was asleep for so many years. I am trying to say something about love and the choices I didn't realize I was making, what I did to survive. I do not have friends from high school; no boyfriends, girlfriends, barely crushes. I was a different kind of queer kid than the kind I've heard about in stories. Being in the diaspora didn't expedite my understanding of my sexuality, myself. It deferred it. I couldn't love or desire anything, not even being alive, for a very long time.

Beit Sahour 1994

In the seventh grade, S tutored me in Arabic. She was an intimidating teacher, taller than most of the other women at our school, big features and a voice that projected. She had soft brown hair in big curls and bangs that gentled her face. She was easy to disappoint, hard to impress. I would come to her house, where she lived alone, and we would sit at the table in her kitchen. She had a kelly green gas stove, and during our sessions she would make me hot cocoa. She was kinder here, at home, than she could be at school. We would go over grammar and mechanics, all the things I did not know as a transfer from an English system to an Arabic one. My Arabic was that of a heritage speaker, and I had to catch up to my classmates in every way. I didn't have the language, I hadn't gotten my period, I couldn't take what I knew of math and make it work in Arabic, I didn't have crushes on my classmates, I didn't spend time on my appearance. I felt childish in many ways, though my childishness would not survive long.

S cold-called on me during class. It made sense; just the night before we had gone over the form of المصدر (al Masdar), a noun derived from a verb. Masdar names an activity or action, the act of doing. Masdar is drawn from the same root word as the verb, which describes the action. So كتب (katab) becomes الكتابة (al Kitaba), كلام (kalam) becomes الكلام (al Kalam). For English speakers, Masdar can be a challenging form as it often appears as a gerund, what in English is a verb. I had understood it the night before but froze in the moment when asked to define it. Instead of starting with Masdar as اسم (ism, noun), I called it كلمة (kalima, word). The rest of the definition jammed. I couldn't self-correct or get past the mislabel. Eventually she gave up on me and asked another student. I could feel her surprise, disappointment. So often teachers assume students have not studied, but she knew I had. She did not take into account my shyness, my insecurity, my easy shame. To shame: أفضح (ifdah). The shamed: المفضوحة (il mufdooha). The shame: الفضيحه (il fadeeha).

Shame was a running currency in our classroom. Once our science teacher brought up all the students who didn't turn in their homework to the front of the class and slapped our palms with a ruler. The students around me seemed used to it, the ways we were made vulnerable by our instructors, the expectation that our failure be known to all, our successes hardly worth mention. I could not disappear in my classes, not only because I was a "foreign" student, an "American," but additionally because I reliably knew less than the people around me. In my experience in the US, high-achieving students were often mocked, their braininess inverse in proportion to their coolness. This was not the case in Palestine. Here, the smartest students were also the most beautiful, the most popular, the most envied. I wanted to breathe that air. I wanted to breathe. I kept going back to S's kitchen all year. The dissonance between her at home and school became normal. S and her double.

From S I learn that the double noun is a distinct grammatical formation from the plural: المثنى (al Muthanna) (incidentally, the Masdar of the verb تثنى (tuthna)). From the double noun comes the double adjective and the double verb. Arabic can construct an entire world for two. It makes sense then, that Muthanna can also refer to the relationship between a pair, their intimacy. Munir Fasheh, a decolonial Palestinian theorist and educator, considers Muthanna an Arabic concept which can address facets of Palestinian culture untranslatable. He writes:

> I always felt I am made up of muthannas. Muthanna refers to a relation between two people that becomes

> very important in their lives, and yet has a life of its own—almost like a common baby. It is neither a legal relationship nor intellectual nor economic nor social; it develops in a free and natural way between the two. It is neither a couple nor dual, although the latter is usually used to refer to it. Each person remains who s/he is, but a relation starts developing between the two which becomes impossible for both to live without feeling it and aware of it.

To be in relation to someone in such a way that their being is fundamental to one's own. To be composed of these doubles, to *always* be in relation to one another. Me and S, a double. Me and D, a double. Me and my family, a double. Me and Palestine, a double. Us, kaleidoscopic multitudes.

Michigan 2002

My sister got engaged right around the end of my college years. Here's what I remember: wearing a beaded black dress in the church hall, watching her dance with her fiancé in the middle of the room, my father leading the call and response, dancing, singing, laughing. I knew in my gut I wouldn't ever be in that position. I wouldn't have a big Arab wedding, a zaffa. I thought, wrongly, it was unlikely I would meet a person my parents would like. I felt, wrongly, that my desire for a certain kind of feminist self was at odds not only with my family but with Being Palestinian. In her work on immigrant families, feminist scholar and activist Nadine Naber writes that immigrants often attempt to secure their heritage in the face of whitewashing or assimilation through gendered and sexual norms. I lived this, the idea that my non-normativity disqualified my Palestinianness. That I could only have the latter (Palestine) if I accepted the norms of the former (heteronormativity). At the party, I kicked off my shoes to dance. I was there and not. A call unanswered, a dabke undanced. At home and undone by it.

Ohio 2006

My first queer relationship came unexpectedly. I was a TA in his section of Intro to Women's Studies. It wasn't as scandalous as it sounds. G was older than me and he asked me out when classes ended and grades were in. A mutual friend of ours said he was always asking out straight women. I joked that I was the one he'd successfully recruited. He had soft hair that flopped over his forehead, brown eyes that deepened with intensity, lightened with humor. He was lanky and I felt myself wanting to fold into him, to exist only inside the landscape of his limbs. We were together around a year before his desire to be in an open relationship and my move out of state undid our togetherness.

I met G during a time in my life where I'd felt increasingly alien from my Palestinian culture. This was expressed as alienation from my parents and birth family and upheld by my distance from Palestine. When I met G, I hadn't been to Beit Sahour in about eight years. I felt out of sync with home since that last visit. I wasn't like my friends there. I didn't want to get married, I didn't want to have kids, I didn't want to live with my parents. I left my family home for grad school and I liked living alone. I didn't know how to reconcile this version of myself with the version I saw in the eyes of my parents, my family, our community.

G cooked big Italian meals and wrote poetry. He got two kittens we'd watch run around his apartment like tiny dinosaurs. We'd sit in the window bed and make promises we were both too young to keep. I hurt him and he hurt me. I loved him and he loved me. I experienced myself in a way I hadn't before. I learned to look even though I didn't understand what I saw.

Michigan 2010

It was summer and we threw a queer prom. We hung twinkle lights in the living room and made a photo booth. We spiked punch and hired a DJ. I was wearing a sleeveless dress with a black sweetheart neckline, a hot pink empire waist, and a pink and black checkered skirt. I pinned flowers in my hair. L came dressed like Carrie, in a white sheath dress, complete with fake blood and tiara. In the photo booth, she'd only take photos with her hands raised at her sides, face turned up in a fake scream. She had a twisted humor, a way of moving through the world that delineated what was serious and what ought not be. My crush on her was expansive; I admired her politics, her uncompromising ethics. I admired her work, her work ethic, her no-nonsense attitude. She was affirming and challenging. As a light-skinned person who frequently passed, I had a difficult time understanding myself as a person of color. She taught me to think of race beyond ontology, to narrate my position with regards to power. Her certainty against my indecision, the clarity of her vision. A crush is an understatement. I loved her.

She was queer and had been out for a long time. She was explicit that she wasn't interested in anyone who wasn't out to their families. That she wouldn't deal with secrecy. I know I disappointed her this way. Being out didn't mean the same thing to me; I felt differently about what parts of myself I made accessible to different people. I didn't have the same kind of queer knowledge about my childhood self that she had. I had come to queerness in my twenties. My relationship to the way it was rendered in the West, through categories like lesbian or narratives like "coming out," was fraught. I was, perhaps, insecure in my queerness in the same way I was insecure about being a person of color. If I didn't know at a young age, was it real? If I wasn't always recognized as Palestinian and treated as such, was I really Palestinian? I've since learned these authenticating questions are themselves ways to fracture and gate-keep my communities. To produce them monolithically and in ways that serve heteronormativity and white supremacy. But I didn't know that then. I knew that I loved her and that I wasn't enough.

At prom, I was fixated on dancing to "Time After Time." It didn't make a lot of sense—it wasn't the right song for what would have been my prom era, I wasn't particularly enamored of Cyndi Lauper. L asked the DJ to play it and held out her hand. We danced. I felt the moment as it passed: what I wanted against what I thought I could have. She went home a little later. I found myself at the end of the night on a porch with a stranger. The wrong kiss, but the one I believed I was allowed. L and I were friends for a long time, until we weren't. Until she was with someone like she was not with me. A chapter that ends with *what if.*

July 2010 Palestine

During a visit back to Palestine after an eleven-year absence, I reached out to some queer Palestinians I'd met through an online queer Arab community. I met R for coffee at a café in Beit

Lehem; she lived in the '48 and it was easier for her to come to me. She had short black hair cut like a Ken doll and a thin-lipped, quick smile. She had those knife sharp Arab girl eyebrows, one pierced. Her voice fast and fluid, she was at home here, at ease asking for things from the barista, confident in her queerness and in the work she did. We smoked Camel Lights and I worried it wasn't appropriate for me to write about queer Arab culture because I didn't live in Palestine anymore, that maybe my position in the diaspora made me an outsider. This was the first time we'd ever met; she took my hand across the table and told me that questioning myself, my vulnerability, suggested that I was the right voice, or at least one of them. She gave me what I ought not have needed but did: permission to be Palestinian and queer, queer and Palestinian.

Here & Now

Strangers on the internet tell me if I lived in Palestine as a queer person I would be murdered. They are so obsessed with killing, accusation as confession. We are living in the genocide. I bolt awake in the middle of the night and check the news. How many of our people have died? I want to describe what it feels like for the world to end every minute. The hollowness in my heart as I learn how little "Americans" know about love. Can you love someone if you can watch the genocide of her people without saying, doing ... anything? In the passing months I've installed a keypad on my heart. I learn who to let go, who to hold close. We write letters, make calls, send money, plan actions. On campus we hold events and speak Palestine and defend the students. None of this is enough, but nothing could be. Palestinian artist Areej Kaoud writes المقاومة أعمق أشكال الحب (Resistance is the deepest form of love.) Palestine asks us to love every day. It tells us that our relation to one another is sacred and exceeds its own form.

I think of my aunt making all my favorite meals when I'm in Beit Sahour. My father drawing my partner to me as we dance in the living room. Every "الله يرضاه عليك" the hajja utters at the market. I think of our arms interlocked around the encampment as the police approach. The fundraiser for Gaza at the local queer space. The echo of "intifada revolution" across thousands. The keffiyeh hailing new kin. The stone against the tank. Our brothers in arms. My doubles. My beloveds. The kind of love we have is boundless. Intifada—the refusal to disappear. Intifada—our love of the land and one another. Intifada—our future inevitable.

Sharts Poetica

by George Abraham

When, come dessert time at the fanciest two-hundred-dollars-a-fish restaurant, I look her in the eyes — daughter of the former CFO paying for dinner — and say, *Got yourself a nice skid mark on your plate there.*

The dish was French, which is to say, I've already forgotten its name. The French value compression, and to them, I gift the wrath of a thousand (and one!) Arab bowels.

Excess like, going back to al-Shidyaq's days, where a seven-page-long list of Arabic words for genitals follows the proem to a 2,000-page novel though, at its center, the project was always about an unraveling, infinite grief.

This and resisting the colonially mediated consequences of standardizing the Arabic language—its operative logic being a cleansing of language, a reduction of tongues.

A century later, when Sonallah Ibrahim was imprisoned for his Communist activism in Nasser-era Egypt, he compressed the notes preceding his post-prison PTSD novel into the space of cigarette papers. After being released and writing the novel, he titled it *That Smell*, referencing a scene where a fart wafts in and disturbs a bourgeoise's morning coffee.

The vulgar is where the compressed meets the infinite, as body meets its own mythologization.

Decades later, when the Egyptian Ministry of Culture awarded Ibrahim the Arab Novel Award, he refused the prize, "for it was awarded by a government that lacks the credibility to bestow it."

I can't think of a single American who has rejected, say, the violence of state-sanctioned book awards, poet laureateship, etc., on the grounds of the illiteracy that is the US government.

Dreaming of one day *pahking my cah in hahvad yahd*, by which I mean, squatting & dropping a No. 2 in front of god and everyone, calling it my (aesthetic) intervention.

When, in the space of another wealthy university that pays their grad students below-poverty-line wages, I thanked the Palestinian for bringing poems with teeth into the space. How he responded, *It isn't that western poetry is apolitical as much as the poems have been cleansed of a politic.*

E.g. searching for a volta like John Donne writing a poem that isn't, somehow, about Bottoming for the Lord.

Searching for the uncleannest poem to toss into the slush pile of another stegner fellow humbled-to-be-wells-fargo-amazon-LOVEISLOVE-industrial-complex-nationally-endowed poet's wet dream.

Titles include: Crapitalism. Hoe de Toilette. Total eclipse of the shart.

At the end of my sharting

there was a floor.

But where does a shart begin, really? At the doorway between ass and toilet? In the second mind of the gut, resisting dairy? At the moment the milk exits the tunnel of a throat? When fluid meets tongue, like a forbidden fruit gushing against the gnash of bared teeth?

Shart, the temporality of my living. That which was once solid, ending in liquid, liquid death.

Is the gut, then, a bridge between the mind and heart, or a critique of the mind/heart division?

E.g. when my father's heart did not kill him, his mind did. The small flare of his stomach saved him from his heart attack, but by the time he passed decades later, his brain was incapable of processing hunger.

My stomach issues began around then, too, my mother told my 28-year-old self, *the doctor said it was ulcerative colitis ... Which I'm just now realizing is genetic ... Whoops!* To know this, my mother's souring center, as a casual inheritance.

The way, after I walked my mother's dog around the apartment complex four times, she ran into my friend's apartment &, within seconds, squatted & dropped the biggest matcha soft serve in the middle of her new rug. All night thereafter, the dog trembled & couldn't leave my shadow.

I call her shart nugget & she only knows how to love me through excess: a little tongue leaking into the border of my ear canal, a sleepy curl at my side, while I read books about the end of the world. How she'd pull me from the trance of words with the nastiest silent but deadly —

Writing poems is like pooping, Sarah Kay told me this at a formative moment. *Sometimes it flows out of you like lava, other times you need to strain yourself to force it out.*

E.g. the prose poem as a poem of infinite line length until *****sharts in register*****

To know the disgust over a line about sharts as the kind of disgust Americans feel in their guts when they look at a body like mine. How I am seen as dirty before I've even opened my (*yikes!*)

Whereas, the only Arab-ness I have ever known was a kind of cleansing.

Olive trees, etc.

My father, in life, glaring at dogs the way our neighbors would look at him.

Let me be the Dirty Ayrab Faggot in an American's mind, if only for a moment.

Whereas instead of knowing queerness as a kind of filling — flesh hardening into flesh, glass slipping into a mucoused surface — I have only known queerness as a need to be emptied.

Not expulsion, but its hollowing *after* — not confession, but its hallowing *after* —

Every word has a hole even if it cannot be seen, heard, or moved through.

If meaning, as Etel Adnan reminds us, is ephemeral then doesn't it follow that our vulgarities are doubly ephemeral?

How evolution returns us to im/permanence.

Once, a man held my poems like a vulgarity. Called hot-mouthed the speaker chasing the infinite excess of their body.

I was raped in the poem. My body, compressed before I even opened my mouth.

In a different memory, a stranger (a gentleman) penetrated me so deeply, I had to leap up from the bed, lunge just to make it to the toilet in time to no 1 + 2 + 3 all in a matter of moments.

To *wet dream* the nightmare.

When I returned, he was laughing to himself. How his own bodily excess triggered simultaneous excesses from the depths of me. How he didn't even feel the need to cum after that.

Or maybe we were both trying to touch the infinite in our bodies. Poetry gave me that, once.

The very real, living correlation between the compression of poems and the compression of bodies.

Headlines, etc.

Lucky for me, most twinks and other size queens wouldn't even look twice at someone like me. I prefer it that way, I think: to be a monster in the minds of men who cannot digest my body, let alone its mauled excess, its expulsions.

Vanessa tells me, *poetry's compression means there's more at stake in language*. Is my gravitation towards excess a need to find safety in (or despite) a language like English?

E.g. how I've compressed my father into example here. How he's appeared only as harbinger, thus far, in the body of this text.

In life, my father would sleep in the living room. Shielded by his snores and the blaring television, I'd sneak into the kitchen, scavenging for snacks to accompany me on sleepless nights: nights of my closeted youth, living next door to the Mormon boy who would not let himself kiss me — nights which translated into sleepless returns to my father, after I escaped from that which he called his home.

Toward the end of his life, he'd wake and catch me full-handed. He'd make me eat the food, there, in his line of sight from the living room to the kitchen, because food in the bedroom was the easiest way to attract cockroaches and he'd never tolerate me filthying his house.

Night after night after his passing, I'd come back to the kitchen — the living room, quiet as a closet without him. I'd grab entire boxes of Cheez-Its, meals of leftovers, and return to my room, hoping some cable would trip me, or some cockroach would reveal itself from an unknowable dark, or some circuit would break, or some light fixture would rattle, or somehow I could tempt his ghost from the silent *non* of its —

Or perhaps, my father makes the most sense as a silent ghost — his youth beneath the shade of a just-drawn curtain, which translated into the small inquisitor of his outline in the window on nights I'd return past curfew.

Beneath my father's gaze, my only safety was food and poetry — my need for language entangled with my need for consumption.

Or maybe, he is less a silent ghost than an oversaturated spectral excess, that lingers beneath towers of suitcases, financial records, and useless technologies of his dead parent's generation, piling up in his attic, spilling into the garage, spilling into the house itself.

A generation before them, our family archive became ash beneath the *non* of a Palestinian landscape. Now, our living are left to filter their descendants' excess and name that which survives, *History*.

Some histories need to die, a mentor said that once.

Years before my father's death, I found a pile of old photographs alongside my grandparents' wedding album — photographs of unknown ancestors in a field, dressed up in thobes and other Indigenous garb. Shortly thereafter, Susan's #TweetYourThobe campaign went viral, with Palestinians worldwide tweeting pictures in thobes, celebrating Rashida Tlaib's inauguration in our Indigenous dress.

Just before taking pictures to tweet, my father accosted me: *is this even your image to own? These, our dead, who cannot give you any permission? And who, exactly, would you be sharing their images to, let alone, for?*

I could ekphrasis them, instead. I could come to the page, as I have now, a dis/obedient son, betraying my father's every need for secrecy: the Arabic he told me never to speak beyond his front door — every secret he fought with his whole life to keep swept away in the dust of his hoarded excess: the 3amo who —

the door where —

I come to the page and must choose between gatekeeper or hoarder of excess — choose between becoming an Acceptable American Poet or becoming my father.

I want to break this binary. I want to expel this, instead.

My relation to Palestine is less one of blood or land, but of grief, Alessandra writes me.

We met at a research talk where I presented on Adnan's *The Arab Apocalypse*, and she presented on Samira Badran's *Twenty Five Barrels*, speaking of the painting's compositional treatment of excess: the fleshy macro-forms of the painting being entirely composed of garbage—the compression of Palestinian bodies, and entire modes of living, in the shadow of Zionist settlements festering in the West Bank.

Adnan teaches us language, itself, can become catastrophe. Badran teaches us catastrophe is, itself, a kind of language.

E.g. keys, American attics, *olive trees, etcs*, etc.

In the current state of American letters, most poetry is just confession without craft, a friend overhears from an editor at one of the US's wealthiest institutions.

My first impulse was to say confession is the opposite of craft: how else to write with a state, or other gun, to one's temple?

Craft, like confession, is a set of expectations, but one that a poet can own, navigate, resist, remake. Confession is the opposite of *owning* language, confession is the compression of self into Good Citizen. The opposite of control.

E.g. suppose the metaphor isn't *poems are poops* but *poems are sharts.*

Write the poem you are most terrified of writing. I gave this prompt to my students, recently. A class later, I told them I was trying but failing to write a poem about sharting.

The poem could have been about my mother — how, at the height of her alcoholism, she sharted in my car on the way home from a morning run on more than one occasion. How it took my father's death for her to get sober. How, while going through initial withdrawal symptoms, all her gut could do was thank her.

How my mother and I had opposite grief responses in our bodies: she cleansed her gut, while I filled mine to break my body into a small god of excess.

The poem could have been about the dog my mother could have never owned while my father was alive — how everything Mama mothers touches turns into a shart nugget. How the dog has made a habit of shitting on my father's favorite rugs.

In every attempt, the attention of the poem led back to my father, back to excess.

Or perhaps, my sharting was never about my mother, or the dis/

inheritance of my father's excess, but was always about attention: how six months on an ADHD medicine left my guts bleached from the inside. How the most successful cure to my mind came at the expense of my gut.

During my neurological tests, the moment my psychiatrist confirmed the diagnosis was my reading test. *You're in the bottom half of the lowest 10ᵗʰ percentile in reading speed,* she said, *in a dataset comprised of high school students...*

She constellated the test to my early language upbringing. How my primary caretaker was my Arabophone grandmother, who passed away at a critical stage of my development: a stage when I couldn't distinguish between Arabic and English, when my father would have to socialize the English into me within a Florida landscape after his mother's death.

Everything is in the language we use, says Layli Long Soldier. What to make, then, of the language that lives in my gut *because* it cannot linger in my mind? Are fragment and excess the only languages which can *stay* in my body?

Often, the last word of a poet's first book is indicative of a larger wound with which the writer will wrestle for their whole life. I read this in a tweet once.

Stay. The last word of *Birthright* is *stay*. The poem was about my then-living father, who watched the book release but didn't live long enough to read it.

Suppose, then, the entirety of my writing revolves around the question of what it means for a Palestinian body to *stay* anywhere? What it means to find language in a body of perpetual expulsions?

E.g. thick lines save lives. Thick lines save lives until—

I know no name for *love* besides *staying*. And the most primal wounds of my body have been the result of a kind of staying, despite. *Love is a supreme violence*, Etel wrote that in a conversation in a novel reckoning with loving Palestinians im/possibly.

If you're still reading me, I want you to stay. I want you to stay, despite my body.

On a phone call a month after my diagnosis, my psychiatrist said she wondered if my reading disorder, itself, was what led me to poetry — a need for compression in a language of excess, a need for breath in a mind that can only process language as a kind of spiraling.

Whereas western poets say *compress,* which implicates the body of text in its own excess, I prefer the Arabophone poetic obsession with *distillation*: that to write a poem about a horse means to distill language into the very essence of a horse, ridding language, im/possibly, of its every impurity.

Whereas compression is a process of self-imposed claustrophobia, distillation is a process of chemical mutation — a process that does not hide its violence, but that also does not implicate, let alone confine, the body. Whereas distillation makes excess a necessity, compression makes inwards-directed stigma of every body of excess. How else to touch the infinite, in our bodies, besides failure of?

Internal question: is it possible to cleanse my poetic praxis of the impurities of American expectation? Is every attempt thereof merely performance?

Unlike English, which punishes run-on sentences, Arabic tends to operate on the punctuation logic of a comma — it is common, for instance, to experience paragraphs as an accumulation of unpunctuated sentences, connected by little more than a particle.

In English, punctuation is not merely a border between sentences, but is a signifier of affect within language. In Arabic, affect must exist independent of text, left completely to be gestured towards within the horizon of the body.

Like history, some poems need to die, and that death can happen only in the body.

I know no ending for this aside from my body.

I know no ending besides

,

Further Thoughts on Living

by Noor Hindi

In the middle of having sex,
she asks:
what's your attachment style?
*
By Wednesday I am loose change
in someone's stupid pocket.
*
Over the last two weeks, how often
have you been bothered
by any of the following problems?
*
Confession: When I tell her
you feel like home
I mean to say
I used to live in a home
that mimics your violence.
*
Poets are fucking annoying.
Me most of all.
I am literally tired of talking
about desire.

★

When I say desire
what I am talking about is the absence
of tenderness.
★

Thoughts that you would be better off
dead, or of hurting yourself.
★

My attachment style is promising Allah
I'll stop writing love letters
to the hoes and then writing love letters

to the hoes.
★

Correction: I am the ho.
★

Correction: I tell a ho
I got that dog in me
so she takes me out back
and shoots me with a gun.
★

Correction: My mother wants to know —
Am I a ho?
★

The first time I had sex
with a woman it was because she wanted me
to help her with her MFA applications.
★

My aunt tells me:
Sex is lying in the dark and waiting

for it to be over.
⋆
Sometimes, it hurts.
⋆
By it I mean everything that has ever happened
and everything we are trying to save.
⋆
Feeling down, depressed, or hopeless.
⋆
All the women in Dearborn are gay
with good husbands
with good jobs
and I think they are cowards.
⋆

Correction: I wanted to be their daddy.
⋆
Correction: I became a failed
experiment, instead.
⋆
When I say queer
I am talking about public safety.
⋆
When I say lesbian
I am pointing to a lack of choice
and the publication
of my body.
⋆
Given the choice between the pen and the knife,
what do you choose?

*

If this is a question you are considering
or have considered
you have chosen the knife.
*
What I am talking about is the privilege
of being the wife of an ugly husband.
*
What I am talking about is the burden
of Arab girlhood daddy trauma.
*
Correction: Let me be your failed
experiment.
*
I loved pinning her against the wall
and fucking until her screams
silenced her shame.

*

Who is the woman sleeping next to me?
At night, I mistake the mirror for ancestry.
*
It is not the men I grieve, but my father's tears
at my brother's wedding as he held me and said:
3o2balek.
*
Feeling bad about yourself or that you are a failure
or have let yourself or your family down.

*

You move past the architecture of fear
when you decide to become your own beautiful city.
*
Example: When my brother asks me
if I am gay
I turn every streetlight on.
*
Example: When my lover wakes me
in the morning, I think:
Mashallah her naked, Mashallah her lips.
*
I bless our ruined hearts. I bless our hunted
flesh.
*
My attachment style is trying
not to make a country out of you
and then making a country
out of you.
*
Linger longer love —
I love you most in the seconds before
I am denied entry.

*

I keep writing about dogs
because my gender is a good boy
who will pay for your dinner
if you are pretty.

⋆

Some of you advocate for a Free Palestine
while walking into that same infrastructure
that makes you bleed.

⋆

By some of you I mean me too.

⋆

By Palestine I mean I am yelling
hello? hello? hello?
on a disconnected line
while my fingernails
bleed.

⋆

Sometimes, I think:
I could have married him — the boy
who wrote me love poems
and slow danced with me
in the dark.

⋆

The way he looked at me —
eyes smooth as lavender —
is the way I catch myself
looking at her.

⋆

By Friday, I am a dog
on a leash walking itself
through a very large park.
The sun is shining
and you cannot see my face.

★

Trouble concentrating on things, such as reading
the newspaper or watching television.
★

I love her as one might love any distant land
I approach but do not enter
I forgive her her fears
I speak of her beauty as if it is a dying thing
★

When the white bitch on Hinge tells me
I'm not really into politics
I consider, for a moment, still fucking her.
★

Does the question of Palestine
have to keep coming up?
Does the question of Palestine
have to keep
coming up?
★

Later, I dream
she is choking me.
★

Later, I'll watch her in slumber. Her tenderness
a country. Her tenderness
an absence I have yet to grieve.

Body and Space (2023-2025)

by Al Maqdisi

"Body and Space" is a photography project that explores the relationship between the individual and their surroundings. Inspired by daily life, this work focuses on individual experiences and their entanglements with the collective as well as the structures that surround them, both visible and invisible.

The series, which examines the relationship between Palestinians and their environment was created across Palestinian villages and cities impacted by the 1948 ethnic cleansing: including (and not limited to) Jerusalem, Haifa, Lifta, and the Jericho mountains. The work considers the structures that shape movement, belonging, and the lived experience of place.

Reckoning

by Sara Solara

The air burns.

The earth quivers.

The hornet trembles.

The sound waves of an explosion reverberate between the hornet's antennae. She burrows in the center of a date palm tree to take cover, nestling between its leaves. Smoke suffocates her minuscule lungs. The chemicals light her airways afire. Toxins sink into her bloodstream and make her woozy. Her muscles have atrophied, her body weakened over weeks without enough nourishment.

Can't breathe. Can't move. Can't lift a wing.

For days on end, giant flying machines, exploding objects, and helmeted humans in dark olive green uniforms have disturbed the land. Burning poisonous gases have seeped into the soil. The red anemone blooms and sweet strawberry bushes have died off, the guava trees withered away.

There is no sustenance in sight. There is only danger and death. The hornet resents the destruction, furious enough to fight, but she hasn't even been able to find a fruit to wrestle over. As the ripples of the explosion fade, her antennae twitch. She shelters between the palm leaves and listens.

There is a rustling in the earth deep below—an energy that flows from the ground, emanates through the tree, and pulses through the hornet's body in a raging rhythm. She can hear echoes of its source, the distorted cries of thousands of souls agitating to break into this realm. With each drop of blood absorbed in the soil, the land groans anew. It is as if the earth is collapsing in on itself, unable to withstand so much pain. The palm tree shudders.

The hornet fears she cannot go on. The lingering poisons cloud her sense of smell, making it impossible to sniff out fresh nectar. But she must try. She will fight with all her ferocity if she must. When the sun at last emerges, the glow warms her body enough that she can summon the strength to take flight.

The hornet soars over the mountains of rubble, traveling far in hopes of finding a blossom to rest on and sip sugary nectar from. She crosses over the barbed wire metal wall that entraps this bombed land, only to fly into more acrid smoke. Dark clouds billow over a forest engulfed in flame on the horizon. The invasive pine trees, those that do not belong to this land, have caught fire in the tinderbox of the dry desert heat, forcing her to flee.

Panic consumes her. The hornet circles haphazardly over the land, drained and disoriented. She has no idea where she's going. She must escape the smoke if she is to survive. She must find clear, untainted air to breathe. She must scout out water and some form of nourishment before her wings collapse.

She flies as fast as she can for hours on end, until she crosses over the tall concrete wall and recognizes her surroundings again. There is a natural spring nearby that she has visited before to sip cool water. She soars toward it in desperation, but when she arrives, even this simple spring has been destroyed—the flow of water cut off.

It is impossible. She knows there are humans who have maintained the spring all her life. What happened to them? Who did this?

As the hornet flies away, she is on the verge of giving up. Surely she will die. She will drop dead in midair, yet another casualty of this destruction. But as she descends, the sudden scent of sweet, succulent grapes finds her.

She doesn't find the grapes herself—her olfactory senses are far too damaged by toxins to detect the sublime hint of sugary fruit on the breeze. Rather, the grapes find her. They draw her into their cool, cozy sanctuary. The hornet lands clumsily on the vine, stumbling, and ducks under the shade of a leaf. Finally she can sink her mandibles into the flesh of a ripe fruit and slurp its juices with her tongue. Sweet relief at long last.

She is not the only hornet sheltering in this vineyard. The more she sniffs and looks around, the more she detects other hornets who feast on the grapes hidden in the shade of the vines. Hundreds of hornets. She greets them, releasing friendly pheromones, and she's welcomed into the hive in return.

The hornet rests there for days, her thorax wing muscles aching from the long journey. She still fears danger, for at any moment a deadly explosion or raging wildfire could sweep her up in its destructive path. But her body is too frail to keep a lookout. She must depend upon her newfound hive to guard her. She dozes.

She stirs only when the sound of a soothing voice tickles her ears, followed by the soft scent of lavender perfume. Under the shimmering sun, a young woman treads between the rows of vines and whispers to the plants. She prunes a vine with the gentlest touch of her fingertips, and then runs her thumb along the white grapes, coaxing them to ripening. The plumpest grapes, she plucks from the vine and collects in her basket.

As the lavender-scented woman approaches, the hornet shudders and hides beneath the grape leaves. She is prepared to sting if her haven is disturbed, if this human intrudes on her space or threatens her existence. She will defend her own life—and mobilize the whole hive if she must. But the young woman simply pauses, plucking a few bunches of grapes while leaving behind the bunch the hornet has been feasting on. Interesting. This human shares the fruit with the hornets, mindful of their presence.

As she should. Fruit is a labor of its pollinators, and the hornets need sustenance if they are to continue the work. The hornet calms, allowing her stinger to rest. There is something about the young woman's presence that feels oddly comforting. A gentleness to her movements, a softness to her spirit. She carries a sorrow deep within, a pain that cannot be healed. It is a familiar anguish.

Ah. It is oh so *familiar. She, too, has been harmed by the destroyers of this land.*

"You are safe here, dear ones," the young woman who smells of lavender whispers to the hornets. "Drink."

The hornet crawls to the next grape, sucking its sweet juices through the tip of her tongue, and drinks her fill until her abdomen is nearly bursting. She rolls under a leaf, heady with sugar, and falls into a deep sleep.

She has nothing to fear here. The human caretaker of this land means no harm, and the hive protects her without a second thought.

When the lavender-scented woman returns a day later, she brings another woman with her. They giggle in soft tones, sneaking quick glances and shy smiles at one another. They wander between the rows of the vineyard and pluck grapes from each side—always leaving behind enough of the harvest for the hornets. At the end of the row, the lavender-scented woman comes to a stop. Her brown eyes dance with mischief.

"Habibti, you must try these."

She holds out a small bunch of the plumpest champagne white grapes, and one by one she feeds them to her mate by hand. The other woman closes her eyes, savoring the sweetness. Upon feeding her the last grape, the lavender-scented woman leans in close to trace the edge of her mate's lips. Their foreheads touch, and her mate's eyes flutter open. They close the gap and kiss under the dappled sunlight in the vineyard.

An undisturbed scene frozen in time. A love worth protecting.

In that moment, the hornet resolves to defend the human caretakers of this land. If not for the vineyard they've cultivated, if not for the hive that pollinated it, she never would have survived the violent attacks. She would have succumbed to dehydration and exhaustion long ago, left to decompose into the earth.

So when the lavender-scented woman rushes out of her home at dawn the next morning, panting in panic, the hornet looks up on full alert to see what has alarmed her. The woman runs off at full speed. The hornet follows, signaling others in the hive to come along.

The lavender-scented woman races down the path to a neighboring home where sturdy olive trees grow. Helmeted humans in uniform have knocked the door down and dragged her mate onto the gravel path. Blood drips from the top of the woman's forehead, trailing down the side of her face, with her body bruised all over. She leans doubled over as if kicked in the abdomen.

Crying out, the lavender-scented woman runs toward her mate. Before she can get close, the helmeted humans who have destroyed this land yell and point their weapons.

Their harsh voices agitate the hornet. She has seen helmeted humans shoot and kill other humans before. Sometimes they drive rolling machines that make explosions, or they round up men and boys to kidnap them in trucks.

Now these destroyers make threatening motions with their weapons, prepared to kill again. The hornet's antennae twitch as their shouts vibrate through the air. The thin sparse hairs on her body bristle.

Other humans from the neighborhood are running up to defend the young woman's mate. There are many people of different ages, from near-younglings to elders. This must be a human hive. The helmeted humans in uniform become tense, swinging their weapons to point them across the coming crowd. To their displeasure, nobody flinches.

Seething, one of the destroyers starts to drag the mate across the gravel toward his armored vehicle. He roughly yanks her by the shoulders.

"Stop it!" the lavender-scented woman yells. "Don't touch her." She charges forward, only for another destroyer to ram into her. This human slams her to the ground.

The hornet flits forward, its wings buzzing rapidly. How dare they hurt the caretaker of the vineyard and her mate? How dare they intrude on this land and kidnap those who love it? How dare they shout and wave their weapons, disturbing the only sanctuary the hornet has found?

Fuck no.

As she zooms closer, the hornet releases an attack pheromone. The hive stirs up in a rage all at once, sensing the offenses these destroyers have committed. Dozens of hornets buzz around furiously, erratic as they close in on their targets. The hornet leads the way, and as soon as enough of her friends have amassed, she divebombs.

She stings the helmeted human who's dragging the mate first, piercing his wrist. Yelping, he jumps back in surprise and drops the mate from his grip. Then dozens of hornets descend on the helmeted humans, who scream in terror. Even more hornets from the vineyard down the road detect the pheromone and soar in, forming a full swarm. The destroyers run for their lives.

Now they are frightened? Every day they wreak havoc on this land, murdering the native humans and polluting their home without any fear of consequence, and now they are frightened by a bunch of buzzing hornets? They have starved and wiped out many life forms, and yet still they imagine they can get away with anything unchallenged. They think they're untouchable.

The hornet pursues the destroyers in a fury, leading a whole swarm bent on vengeance. The destroyers attempt to shield their faces from the stings and run wildly to their armored vehicle, as if they'll be safe there.

The attack pheromone the hornet released has multiplied with the joining swarm. The scent draws curious creatures to the scene, who spring into the fight upon seeing this land's caretakers under attack. Snakes lash out at the destroyers, sinking their teeth into their ankles. Gazelles bound out of the mountains to rush the soldiers. Braying donkeys gallop out of the stable and join the chase. A murder of crows swoops down from the sky and bashes their beaks against the destroyers' helmets.

Cowering, the helmeted humans sneak quickly into their vehicle. The hornet directs some of her friends to follow them inside and repeatedly sting them, until they regret coming to this place. The small piercings of stingers in human skin will be only the tiniest fraction of the all-consuming suffering they have wrought on this land.

The human hive rallies next. Many of them run at the armored vehicle with their garden shovels, leaving big dents, while others use slingshots to crack the front windshield. Then a crow swoops in. The black bird tears the white-and-blue flag off the vehicle and throws it to the ground, where the gazelles immediately trample it.

The armored vehicle roars to life. The destroyers flee, darting around the gazelles before taking off at full speed.

The lavender-scented woman comes to the side of her mate. Tenderly, she wipes the blood from her forehead with a cloth. The mate cries in relief and rests her head on her beloved's shoulder. The human hive quickly surrounds them with care, offering water to drink, a balm to heal cuts, and bandages to mend wounds. Their warm, radiant presence envelops the couple.

The hornet circles the human hive, satisfied that the attackers have run away. The helmeted humans will think twice about setting foot here again. The land that nurtures life has rejected their destruction.

With her work done, the hornet releases a new pheromone to calm her hive. It's time to guide them down for a rest—but not without leaving the couple's side. She flutters to the edge of the roof of the house and lands there. Her newfound hive descends with her, hundreds of hornets landing upon the roof. Their buzzing fades into silence as their wings still. The snakes slither toward the gravel pathway, standing watch, while the crows peer down from a nearby palm tree. The donkeys settle in front of the stable. The gazelles bound back toward the house, and then pause to nibble on the grasses.

Once the lavender-scented woman has bandaged up her mate, she holds her tight and presses light kisses on her forehead. She whispers thanks to her protectors in quiet awe. What has happened feels impossible in the face of constant, catastrophic violence, but no one can kill and destroy forever without reckoning with the land.

La Sombra of Who I Am
R/evolutions (Queer Tatreez)

by Micaela Kaibni Raen

"This land, my sister, is a woman." Excerpt from the poem "Hamza," written by Fadwa Tuqan, as published in *Night and the Horseman*, 1969.

who was my grandmother
what died with her
and is buried in the soil
anciano debajo
the **burning sun**

¿Quiénes eran
mis abuelas
ancianas?
una mujer de los espíritus
a spirit woman
darker than my *zhedu* visits me
compelling me to places within
never thought **to exist**
she knows that I can cook
only **in** a **language** not mine
that I have built my life rebelling
against those uncles
demanding
I was too independent
outspoken
as **I** watched them send from our homeland
for their next wife
she would for them
give freely of her **fertile soil**
sow seeds and govern their growth
become lost **in** Anglo utopia
surrounded by unfamiliar words
and few others like **her**
b(r)ought
from her **homeland**

La Sombra of Who I Am *by Micaela Kaibni Raen*

I
white-skinned opinionated
Queer girl
am valueless to men
I
lesbian (of color
if only deep inside)
am to them *haram*
a freak
I need to **know**
the entirety of what I resist
maybe...I tell myself
it's not as bad as **my** childlike **eyes**
have seen it to be
I have never cooked traditional bread
in a *tabun*
only *warak enab*
on a gas stove
with bottled grape leaves
and lamb meat
bought from the Arab butcher
I **have** no ingrained tolerance for maleness
to lift me to freedom
freedom from men
freedom to cushion my **new realities**
I am unacquainted with tradition
its severity of punishment
for all that is considered
haram
censoring our voices

devaluing our importance
beating us into submission
can I
young lesbian whiter looking
than most Anglos
silence my own voice
succumb to male superiority
so I can **discover** my *hamouleh*
and my grandmothers
if woman only has **power** through man
can I hide my lesbian-ness
my **love** for *todas las mujeres*
can I stop
the burning **desire** for desert women
for love between women
is much more than
haram
it is impossible here
I am what for many women
they are not allowed to **be**
a strong female **warrior**
collecting power
from those whose wings
conquered the great winds
who is this visionary woman
pushing me closer
to meadow **nights' shine**
the **poppies' whispers**
to her **moonlit *Tatreez***
in the web of stars' moon

to her **dance**
my heart's *intifada*
how much of myself
must I sacrifice to satisfy this hunger
to discover, to know
the feathers of women
inside my soul
I am *bint*
soy una niñita del sol
an outsider looking inward
to search for the visionary
Palestinian woman calling to me
the ends of her *thobe*
cascading *Tatreez* tight to fraying tassels
dancing on the sandy soil of my past
¿Es ella ***la Diosa****?*
the **earthmother**
Sappho's messenger
or a culmination
de todas ***mis abuelas****?*
I miss **my** grandmother's hands
watching them
as she washed grape leaves
mixing lamb with lemon juice in a large bowl
watching her **hands**
turn the pages of my **herstory**
to her nightlight as we slept
I in the bed
of my dead grandfather
watching *sus manos*

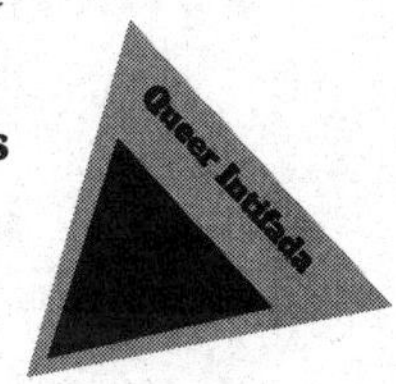

work **endless** crossword puzzles
not **knowing how to love** me
or even if she should
things she loved
had a tendency **to die**
our Arabic language **lost**
as she watched her daughters grow
and marry white men
in the closest of cousins
she had the **reflection** of herself
her son did not marry white
she was my only *teta*
my *zheda*
Umm Richard
and I looked nothing like her **daughter**
todavía la mujer **come**s **to me**
dancing *con la música en mi alma*
I must
to **complete the circles of my life**
follow the visionary *mujer*
wandering **backward**
not forward to find myself
mientras la sombra
of who I am is widening
and soon will be
overtaken by the **darkness**
se desaparece
se oscurece
in night **skies**
as the same **winds**

that once caressed her face
now ancient
hold mine
to the **stars**

My Heart's Intifada

Author note:

Art and poetics are inspired by *Tatreez*, Indigenous Palestinian embroidery and textiles. Bold words comprise a poem in the voice of Queer/Trans Palestinian ancestors.

Legacy

by Eman Abdelhadi

Yahya found out his mom had died like he found out most things about her: from the news.

"New Pioneers Kill Writer and Activist Manal Abdelhadi"

He searched within himself for sadness or anger, but all he found was the familiar weight of obligation. He carried that heaviness to Shikaakwa, imagining he would have to coordinate her funeral, find someone to do her *ghusl*, and recruit an imam to oversee her burial. Old friends confirmed his mother had been working with Assata's Rebels, who had recovered her body. At their headquarters, he identified himself as her son and was ushered into a dimly lit room where two older women stood over her as she lay on a large wooden table.

Manal had already been washed and wrapped in crisp white cotton. One of the women turned to him and he stammered; she was husky and likely in her fifties. He guessed they were both Arab. "Marhaba khalto, ana ibenha Yahya." She nodded and let her eyes linger on his face. He imagined she was looking for Manal in his sallow cheeks. Her gaze moved down his body, assessing him. She would not find Manal in his skinny frame either. A familiar impulse overtook him: the desire to explain himself. *I take after my father. There's no one like her really. El saraha, we aren't—weren't—close.*

Instead, he let his eyes wander around the room. Both women's weapons' belts had been laid carefully on a blue velvet wingback chair in the corner. He wished he could sink into it, curl up and go to sleep. He pictured himself hugging one of the rifles like a body pillow. Maybe he would wake up in a different reality than this one. Finally satisfied—or content in her dissatisfaction—the *khalto* he had addressed nodded sideways towards the body, giving him silent permission to approach.

The swaddled woman looked nothing like the one who had once given him life. There must have been some mistake, he thought, relieved. But her features slowly declared themselves. The high cheekbones. The straight edge of her nose. The curve of her nostrils. The white curls in whisps around her face. She was unmistakable, even in death. He blinked, hovered his hands over her face for a moment, then clenched them back into fists and returned them to his pocket. Once more, he searched in his chest for a feeling, any feeling at all.

She had not needed him to organize a funeral. Tens of thousands took to the streets to follow his mother one last time. Like her life, it was march and protest and riot. The mourners wept in their combat gear, held up weapons and signs bearing her quotes. Here was something she had said, something she had written, something she had shouted into a crowd. Hand drawn and hand painted portraits of her beamed at him with a look he recognized as more hot than warm.

Afterward, Yahya took a boat to the east side of the city and climbed the familiar stairs to her third-floor apartment, lingering at the windowsill to contemplate Michigamaa. The lake had been her great joy. "The lake is the reason to live in Chicago," she'd say, slipping into the city's settler name.

The apartment hadn't changed much in the fourteen years since he'd lived there. The books were still the main characters, his mother's true loves mocking him from their high shelves. He stood before the case lined with her name. There, in chronological order, sat her life's work, everything she had ever written. Every book or article, every opinion piece. At first, the shelves only had print publications. But she had become an archivist of herself in the later years, when the Net started glitching, she would wait for hours by her computer, printing one article at a time whenever she could catch enough signal. Eventually, she even transcribed her old interviews—dozens, hundreds even.

He ran the tips of his fingers over the bindings. Here were her real children, the ones who could not disappoint. The ones whose politics were perfect, who never asked for attention or visits or quality time. They could feed themselves just on others' curiosity.

He thought about packing them all. He thought about burning them all. He thought about picking a few to take. Instead, he walked away.

Emerging from his daze, he pulled her heavy iron bed to the side, popped the familiar floorboard up, and dug for the small red velvet box. "The Iraqis say 'zeena w khazeena,'" Manal would say whenever the subject of the gold came up. "Your great grandfather and grandmother survived the Nakba because they took her gold. They thought they were coming back, but they took the gold just in case."

Gold tucked into his inner pockets, he headed back to Mishigamaa to gather his few possessions. He had not acknowledged it to himself, but she was the only reason he had stayed on Turtle Island. "Good leftists stay and fight," Manal had always said. He did not have the body—or disposition—of a fighter. He lacked his mother's charisma and her intellect—he read nothing and wrote less. No one needed him here. But he could not bear to disappoint her in yet another way. And there was the fantasy that one day she'd need him, a fantasy he nursed by picturing her old and frail and alone and desperately reaching for his care and affection one day. He would come, he had thought, reluctantly. He would feel redeemed—to have finally become useful to her, to prove once and for all that he was the dutiful son she had failed to see. He should have known better. Even in her death, she had proven him useless.

A few days later, he had made it to Lenapehoking, where he climbed onto a refugee ship headed for the Maghreb. The ships were not supposed to exist. Neither rebels nor unionists wanted anyone to leave. But neither side had the bandwidth to stop them.

Soon he was climbing off a different ship on the shores of Gaza.

Palestine, the United Communes of the Levant (UCL)

In Rimal, a group of people in bright green vests awaited him and his shipmates. Yahya was once again grateful that Manal had taught him Arabic. The vests read: Fareeq al Tarheeb—Welcome Team. When asked, he said he'd like to head to Nablus, that he was a returnee whose father was Palestinian and whose mother was half Palestinian. They asked if he wanted to go straight to Nablus or to stay in Gaza, and he elected the latter.

Gaza was a place of myth and glory, the birthplace of Yahya's namesake and the global revolution still underway in Turtle

Island. He had been raised on stories of its resistance fighters, and its triumph over Zionism. Gaza's people, he had been taught, had exposed the rot in the previous world order and had taught the world to struggle.

When he told them he wanted to wander, the Tarheeb team gave him a device with a map and instructions on how to reach his lodgings for the night. He walked for miles along the corniche by the sea, mesmerized both by the glimmer of the Mediterranean to his left and the majesty of the city to his right. Life bloomed all around him. On the beach, people lounged under the sun, picnicked, ran or biked. He had forgotten what it was like to watch people simply enjoy themselves; the war on Turtle Island had left little time or energy for leisure. In Gaza, people lounged under the sun. A group of young people sat in a circle, each holding an identical book, arguing passionately and gesticulating wildly. A group of men in their sixties sat around a table, smoking *argeeleh* and playing cards. Children ran from slide to monkey bar and back in the many playgrounds that lined the walkway. It dawned on him that he had taken a ship into the future.

Waves of delight and anger washed over him. Manal could have raised him here. Much of the Palestinian diaspora in the US had returned in the early '30s after liberation. But Manal had refused. "We have always said none of us are free until all of us are free," she said. "I am not abandoning the fight for Turtle Island and our comrades here." As always, it was hard to argue with her. He suspected, though, that she had other reasons to stay. Over the years, she had pared her life down to the struggle. After she skipped her intended abortion on that fateful day, he had been the only indulgence she had allowed herself. Who would she be without meetings and protests and fiery speeches? He could not imagine that version of her, and he was sure she could not either.

The next morning, he was on a bullet train to Nablus. The city on the mountain looked like his mother's posters and photographs. White buildings grew out of hillsides, punctuated with the greenery of lemon trees, the domes of mosques and crosses of churches. Surrounding the city though were enormous buildings that were clearly newer, their white stone carved with intricate patterns competing with green vines for attention. They looked more like Gaza's buildings, only a few decades old and built to counter the glass-and-steel looks of the twentieth century.

In Nablus, another Tarheeb team greeted him. "Marhaba, ahla w sahla, my name is Anwar or Anwaar—whichever you prefer" a green vest said brightly as they approached him. They had short curly hair that was long at the top of their head and grew shorter and shorter into a fade at the back of their neck. Anwar did not seem to notice how their energy overwhelmed Yahya.

"I'll be taking you to *bayt-el-mesafreen* for a room, and we'll get you a guide there!"

"How much will that cost? I spent most of my gold getting here. I think I need to exchange the rest," Yahya said.

"Exchange it for what?" Anwar asked, tilting their head to the side, face falling with confusion.

"I'm sorry, our Net has mostly been down on Turtle Island because of the war, I couldn't really research the currency."

"Oh!" Anwar finally understood. "We do not use currency exchange here. You're welcome at the Traveler's House for as long as you'd like to stay."

"Who maintains it?"

"The neighborhood communes. Most communes have travelers' buildings for guests and new arrivals. They'll find you a room until you're ready for something more long term."

Yahya nodded, not quite understanding.

Beit-el-mesafreen was an Ottoman-style home with a fountain in a tile courtyard surrounded by rooms and bathrooms. A friendly robot in a tarboosh was washing the floors when they arrived. The house had a small kitchen and a stocked pantry, to which he was told he was welcome, but Anwa(a)r also pointed Yahya to the neighborhood canteen down the road, where bigger meals were served regularly.

"Folks decided they wanted newcomers to start off here in the old city, to get a feel of Nablus, to understand how it came to be Jabal el Nar. A lot of our history is preserved here, and there are many educational and cultural sites. Some folks end up loving it and staying, but most end up moving out to the high-rises eventually. Especially people our age. People feel like there's more energy out there, more density, more going on. The big syndicates are mostly out there too, so depending on how you want to spend your time, it can be more convenient. My love is in the astrophysics syndicate, so we mostly stay out there too. Honestly though, I like it more in the old city. When I need space, I come stay in one of the communes here."

Yahya struggled to take in this monologue. He had a feeling Anwar would continue if he didn't intervene. "I'm sorry, I'm a little tired," he finally eked out.

"Oh!" Anwar giggled and hunched over slightly. "I can just keep talking! Let me show you to your room. When you're ready,

I'll come back and give you a full tour. Here's a tablet you can use to find me or search the net." Anwar showed him how to call or send a message on the strange device, which was much more advanced than anything remaining on Turtle Island.

Finally nestled into a room, Yahya slept through the rest of the day, and the next day, and the one after that too. He slept and slept and slept. On the third night, Yahya finally noticed the quiet. No gunshots. No drones. No sirens. It was the first time in decades he had slept that well.

On the fourth day, he finally messaged Anwar, who was eager to return.

They walked the city, neighborhood by neighborhood. Here was the canteen in Yasmina. There was the creche in Gharb. Here was a library in Qaryun. "You said you're Abdelhadi on one side, right?" Anwar asked. "This library used to be a palace owned by the Abdelhadi family back in the early twentieth century." There was the clinic in Aqaba. And everywhere there were the gardens—on balconies, on rooftops, on the tiniest of lots squeezed between buildings.

Yahya wondered about the small storefronts displaying wares, everything from soap to clay pots to high-tech gadgets. "Are these things for sale?" he asked. Anwar gave him an indulgent smile. "These are craft houses. You can go in and ask for what you need, or you can find one that teaches a skill you want to learn. Most production happens by printer out by the high-rises, but we try to keep the artisan traditions alive, and people like to have some handmade things. How did you spend your time on Turtle Island?"

"Well, I studied chemistry and was going to work in pharmaceuticals. But then the wars started and life got a bit scrambled."

"Well, the universities are open, if you want to continue your studies or enter a new field. Our pharmaceuticals syndicate is always training folks."

When Yahya didn't respond, Anwar just continued.

"Or you can also pick up a craft or work in production. You could go out to the farms. I spent time there during harvest last year. I had been doing robotics maintenance, because I come from an engineering background, but I got a little burnt out and felt like a change. So I went out there ..."

"Tarhib isn't your main job?" Yahya asked.

"Well, I am passionate about community, and I love welcoming new people, so I do Tarhib shifts a few times a month. No one does just one thing here. It would be too painful, too boring, too hard on the body. We all do bits and pieces of what we like."

Yahya nodded. He was struggling to understand the rules of this place, the homeland his mother had trained him to dream of, that she had fought for her whole life and to which she never returned.

"Are there any rules for what you can do?" Yahya asked.

"Yes and no. Some things, you need to learn for a certain amount of time before you can do them. You can't decide to be a surgeon tomorrow, but you could decide to study to be one. And then the medical co-op would put you in classes, you'd take exams and all that. Kind of how it was in the old times, and I think Turtle Island is still like that? But there's no salary at the end, that's the difference. People do it because we need them to, and because they love it. Other stuff is more relaxed. I could teach you to give tours in a week or so, and you could join Tarhib. A lot of people float between jobs based on their interests, their bodies, what else they have going on. Others really want to perfect something, and they study for a long time. You seem like one of those brainiacs who might want to focus up."

Yahya was quiet for a while.

"What if I don't want to do anything?"

Talal laughed. "Everyone from Turtle Island always says that when they first show up. I can't tell if it's the brainwashing they give you there or that you're all just so damn tired. But no one lasts more than a few months before getting into something. It's too boring to sit around."

"What if I never did get into anything?"

"You still don't get it. No one *has* to work, no one *has* to do anything. Most people want to do stuff, they want to contribute, their neighbors and friends and family and comrades are cooking, cleaning, creating—they want to do that too. It's human nature. People want to accomplish, want to be proud, to be able to say 'Hey, I made that! I did that!' Plus people start to feel ashamed if their comrades are carrying them, and they're doing nothing. You'll find your place. Pharmaceuticals is a good place to start."

Again, Yahya nodded, unable to muster a reaction beyond skepticism.

"Wait, I lied," Anwar started up again. "You kind of do have to go to your neighborhood assembly. If you don't, people get really worried and stressed and everyone will scold you. It's social suicide to miss more than a couple. Your friends will stage interventions, people will ask if you need to see a therapist."

"What happens at the assemblies?"

"Everything. They're where co-ops and teams report back to everyone on how production is going, try to recruit folks for jobs that need doing. Coordinators with other neighborhoods or communes will report back there too. It's where we make all the decisions. It's great or it can be a pain in the ass. Everyone loves them, except those on council. You'll hate them when you're on council."

"Me?"

"Oh yeah, that's another thing everyone *has* to do, I guess. At least two terms on council. There's mandatory and elected. If you like being on council—there are weirdos who love it—you can run for a seat. But there's a limit on the number of terms, of course. The main council though is just whoever's turn it is to serve, it rotates so that not everyone leaves at once. It's pretty simple really."

Overwhelmed, Yahya simply nodded.

"Will anyone be joining you here?" Talal asked. "Parents? Siblings? Friends?"

"No, my mom was the only blood kin; she just passed away."

"I'm sorry," Anwar said and looked at Yahya expectantly.

Yahya felt the words rushing up his throat. "Thank you. She was a special person. I wish I knew her better, you know? Everyone seemed to know her better than I did. She was kind of famous. An organizer and a writer back home. She did a lot of Palestine work on Turtle Island and then was advising rebel groups and even fighting during the liberation war ... I'm sure you haven't heard of her here, Manal Abdelhadi. It is so weird to be here; she fought so hard for this place, and she never got to come back. I guess I always thought we'd end up back here together, but I'm here alone. I didn't see that coming, I guess. We weren't close though—"

"Wait. I am so sorry to cut you off. But Manal Abdelhadi? *The* Manal Abdelhadi? *After the Future? The Self in Struggle? That* Manal Abdelhadi?"

"That's her." Yahya braced himself for the familiar flood of pride and shame that washed over him when people recognized his mother.

"Oh wow. I have something to show you."

They walked in silence for forty minutes farther into the old city and stopped at a building that Yahya recognized as the former Abdelhadi palace-turned-library Anwar had pointed out earlier. The plaque outside said "Diwan Ashuhada"—the Martyrs' Forum. Beyond the glass entry way was a cavernous room with mosaic tiles. Stone arches framed the windows, themselves adorned with geometric patterns. The walls were lined with ceiling-high bookshelves. Talal led him to a corner of the room, and there, another plaque. "Manal Abdelhadi," it read in Arabic.

As he stepped in front of the plaque, it lit up. He realized it was a button. He hesitated, but Anwar reached over and pressed it, eager to show him. A screen descended from the ceiling, and there she was. Manal in soundbites. A few sentences from a university lecture, a rally speech, a video interview. On the left hand, a menu appeared. There was her archive, digitized, organized, better than anything she could have done herself. She lived on in the future she had tried to build, the one she'd never actually see.

To Be. Dead. Queer. Trans. Palestinian.

by Mx. Yaffa

My aunt died two days ago on the 20th of May 2025, and I wonder where her hopes and dreams live when she has never been permitted home.

Do they haunt land that she was caged in? Do they haunt people who care about Palestinians except for Palestinian neighbors? Do they live with Mama, also barred from returning home on slightly less hateful land? Do they live with me on stolen land far more racist, thousands of miles away?

I have asked these same questions within different roles for my entire life. I have asked them dozens of times for every queer and trans Palestinian I know who has been killed in Gaza and thousands of times for the thousands of queer and trans Palestinians killed in Gaza I do not know.

The four dozen I did know live within me, hidden even to my own mind as I keep their secrets. I do not yearn to carry these stories, yet I pray that more find me so that at least one person remembers them.

Every day I work to build a world where no one is erased when they are killed, where no one is killed, where hopes and dreams find home like we hopefully find home.

To be a Global Majority queer and trans person generally means we do not have death rites. Because we are trans, we don't even have our names listed in our own memorials at times.

To be a trans Palestinian is to be killed without anyone noticing, even other trans Palestinians. I say this with the frustration of knowing dozens of queer and trans Palestinians killed in Gaza, while the vast majority of queer and trans Palestinians I know in diaspora or occupied Palestine know none.

So I offer this as death rites for all of us who will not have proper rites as we die, either naturally or by assassination.

I say assassination because to be trans is to be politicized whether we want to be or not, and our killing is an assassination.

I light a candle. I burn sage. I drink sage and mint tea. And I breathe in the names of everyone I can remember, a lifetime worth of names, and I exhale into action.

Mourning is a release and a call to action. To grieve without action is to dishonor the dead and the entirety of death itself. Death is a part of the spiral of life; it will always happen. Everything dies.

But we do not merely die today, we are killed—assassinated, by genocide, by preventable billionaire-made diseases, by state violence, by community violence, even from *qahher* (hearts broken due to injustice). And when we are killed, there is always a call to action to build a better world.

I have been doing death work my entire life and officially since I was seventeen, when the vast majority of people I was close to were either killed or disappeared, between the Syrian revolution, Iraq, and various other places around the world where white supremacy kills my people. I learned to move through death out of necessity and as with everything, there was a larger call to action in my responsibility to collective liberation.

I started working with trans asylees and trans unaccompanied minors when I lived on Quinsigamond in the early 2010s. It was a time when I realized that no one else was going to work with us, it was just us—"us" being a subjective term because twelve years later I still don't know anyone else doing that work.

White social workers at the time would both try to keep trans asylees from discovering my Muslim legal name and brownness, and in their desperation would often refer them to me when they realized they did not know what they were doing.

I would meet them, prioritizing children due to my own capacity, and then the white social workers would be shocked that I did not ask about every single death surrounding these children. Instead, we spoke about soccer most of the time. (I am not the type of queer who understands sports, but I did for these kids). The social workers wanted immediate answers; they failed to understand that in my line of work, I will not force anyone to relive the horror they have been put through. People will talk about death when they are ready, but some will never discuss losing their entire family.

There is a myth that we can only heal through naming and processing our wounds. This denies that love and belonging actually heal without naming the inhumane injustice we have experienced. There is no fixing genocide or putting a salve on the wounds of losing every single loved one. There is no going back. I know this, having lost everyone at seventeen. But there is loving and living after. There are still football matches and favorite teams.

And as we move through the spiral of life there is death, more death. But when you've lost everyone due to systemic violence, death is not a beautiful part of the spiral of life; it is injustice that lives in your body through *qahher* and like a cancer spreads and tears your life from you from the inside out.

In Palestinian culture we call *qahher* the silent killer, an emotion beyond rage and pain that lives in our bodies. There is no English equivalent. The closest I can think of is the concept of dying from heartbreak, but the heartbreak here is not a separation of intimate relationship, it is your child being killed in front of you, it is your entire friend group disappearing, it is not knowing how or why your best friend was killed. I reflect on *qahher* throughout my book *Living to 99*, recognizing the importance of understanding this emotion if we are to move through death, collectivism, nonattachment, and towards liberation.

I truly believe that if we process our deaths we would live very different lives. We cannot desire liberation without claiming our deaths as part of the spirals of our lives.

But we can't claim our deaths when we haven't detached them from genocide and addressed *qahher*.

I have worked with many Palestinians since Oct 7, 2023, and death for us has changed entirely since then, similar to how it had changed dozens of times for other people impacted by genocide, and as I witnessed the shift in those who witnessed the brutality of the Syrian regime under Bashar.

I was called in recently to support a Palestinian elder as she died. I was called because her loved ones were concerned about the state of her mental health. What they did not tell me was that she had been diagnosed with stage 4 cancer earlier that week, and when I met with her, she was processing this like anyone would—by thinking about death and wanting to die.

Normally, my work is with the individual dying. Most of the people I work with do not have families and friends around to support and witness them dying. (Yay for Global Majority trans people who are entirely on our own.) But since October 7, 2023, it's rarely the person dying who needs the most support.

Now, watching a single loved one dying is the same as watching all our people dying, and more than any other time I've witnessed people who are unable to differentiate between death and genocide.

Now I support families first, holding space to allow them to process the death of their loved ones and the immense survivor's guilt they carry, as we know this genocide does not end without at least half a million of our people dying.

I wish I could say that I have the capacity to work with dozens of families at a time. In reality I work with one; the rest of my work is with queer and trans Palestinians in and outside of Gaza. There are many death workers out there capable of supporting families, though not enough specializing in genocide and definitely not enough infrastructure to make this work accessible. But I do not know of anyone working on matters related to death or any other area specifically with queer and trans Palestinians in Gaza.

I don't often talk about any of the people I work with on the ground. If you have not claimed responsibility for the collective liberation of queer and trans Palestinians, then you have not earned the right to any of the stories I carry. I am mindful of folks' safety and privacy, but even when folks are okay with me sharing bits and pieces of their stories, I will not, not even to other queer and trans Palestinians. If you aren't supporting us alive, you are not worthy of knowing our stories dead. There is no excuse for not being in relationship with us, I do not care who you are.

I will share one quick story here as a gift within this essay, one of far too many.

I was working with two individuals, one trans, one queer, partners but they do not know I know, and I do not tell them I know for it is irrelevant. I am working to evacuate them both, fundraising, coordinating money transfers, transportation, setting things up for after the border crossing, and so on and so forth. On one of the days of Ramadan at Suhoor, the day they are meant to evacuate, an air strike kills the trans Palestinian and their entire family.

Death is a beautiful thing, but this isn't that. The death of a lover, compounded with the death of entire families, of the attempted erasure of an entire people, and like so many other cases like this one, no one but me knows. No one else cares to know and I will never forgive having to carry these stories alone.

The queer Palestinian evacuates. To this day they do not know that I know the depth of their pain. Unfortunately, even if they read this, they may not recognize themselves because this isn't a single story from the last nineteen months. Too many ended even more violently.

To pretend that death as an entire concept has not shifted is to deny that part of the purpose of genocide is to eradicate life.

In my family, we have always honored death as a part of the spiral of life. Now, my aunt dies and there's a heaviness hovering above the family that I haven't seen in relation to death before.

Her death is directly linked to medical and community negligence. I see the family shutting down, realizing that sometimes it is our people who enforce the injustice that kills us. I realize that sometimes it's those who love us most who harm us the most. In a lot of ways, I think the family is sitting with the realization of having stood by for decades and watched this unfold and did nothing. Now it's too late.

There is no processing injustice and genocide. They are not meant to make sense. There is no level of understanding that makes them make sense. Be grateful they do not make sense. And at the same time we are all capable of harm and injustice. We have all failed our loved ones at one point or another.

A few months ago, as I was recovering from surgery, my sister was watching the news in Gaza around me, and she asked me, "How can anyone be okay with killing people like this?" And I responded, barely able to speak, that most people disconnect from the violence they enact. I gave her our relationship as an example, saying "You know calling me by my dead name hurts me, yet you have been doing it for years knowing that. It's a different scale but the concept is the same." We sat in silence after—no response, no change in behavior.

I wonder what comes next with my family, even as I know from the past that most in the family will feel the weight and never move through it until the next pain and the next pain and, like my sister, will not heed the call to action. I hold hope that everyone finds their way, but I cannot force them, just like I can't force my sister to show up differently.

This same thing is happening globally. Too many are stuck under the weight of genocide, incapacitated and unable to act. Or there is action, but only from a place of wanting to alleviate the pain and lacking a strategy for actually moving to a better world.

When I work with individuals, we discuss mourning as a call to action. We discuss what the action could be and we discuss the individual's role. There is a myth that when you have lost everything, you will always be stuck in the grief, when in reality so many of us become responsible for collective liberation and support others heeding our own call to action and claiming our roles. Everyone I support is a world-builder. I do not have capacity to support others who are not willing to claim responsibility for collective liberation.

In our talks we discuss how the remedy to survivor's guilt is understanding and claiming our roles. Often, survivor's guilt comes from having access to a different life than others who are more marginalized. The remedy is a realization that, having been born in diaspora, my role is different than the role of a trans person in Gaza—it has always been different. My role in responding to the harm my aunt lived through is different from any other family member who carries their own positionality and has entirely different access points than I do.

Finding and claiming our roles is what allows us to move past survivor's guilt and heed the call for action as we mourn. We all have a role to play. Some have had to carry multiple roles because most have not answered the call for action. Until we are able to carry the responsibility of collective liberation together, we will not be able to truly move towards a world where we can separate death from injustice. And until we separate death from injustice, we will not fully claim the responsibility of collective liberation. This sounds like a contradiction, but as with most things related to collective liberation, they happen in tandem—there is no one without the other. There is no step-by-step user's guide for how to move to collective liberation; it is many things happening in tandem that ultimately move us towards a collectively liberated world as we practice it.

Death is a practice. Liberation is a practice. Life is a practice.

When I say practice, I mean that we must rewire our neuropathways to decondition our minds away from systemic oppression conditioning and move towards living liberated lives. We are talking about changing our brain chemistry. When I say mourning is a call to action, I do not mean a single action or a single moment of mourning. I mean that we are always answering the call because to live in this world as it currently exists is to always be in mourning.

Liberation is not something that comes after the fall of systems of oppression; to assume so is to grant these systems power over us—power they do not have but which they pretend they do. Liberation is recognizing our power and that they can never take away our actual power. Liberation exists within an oppressive world. As we claim power, we claim our roles; as we claim our roles, we claim responsibility for collective liberation and vice versa.

Every moment of mourning is an invitation into liberation. We will not move into a liberated world if we continue refusing to answer the call. Mourn everything, answer always, and find liberation everywhere.

I hold hope that someday no one will be caged away from home, a day when injustice is no longer assassinating us. I hold hope that one day we will be in a world where the barriers to claiming liberation no longer exist. I hold hope that one day stories like the ones I carry are rare and far in between, eventually nonexistent. I hold hope that one day we will all have claimed our deaths, and in doing so, claim liberated lives. I believe we will get there regardless. Liberation is ours, within our and every lifetime.

Khalto, may you now find home in a way you never did within these systems.

May the few I have worked with and the many I have not worked with find liberation in this life and every extension of existence.

May we all find liberation. May we all be home.

May the dead rest. May the living rise.

Queer as Ghareeb

by S.

What makes you feel loved as a Palestinian?

The question was posed to me by F, a dear friend and fellow queer Palestinian American, in front of a mostly white audience. This was an early stop on tour for my recently released book, *The Hollow Half*, and outside the DC bookstore, the imperial capital was sunlit and adorned with blooming trees. It was the second spring, the second year, of livestreamed genocide and ethnic cleansing in Gaza. F's question struck me—tender, simple, bold. I opened my mouth and found no answer.

Since October 7, 2023, my Palestinian identity had felt overwhelmingly like a vector of sorrow and rage. This, a familiar falsehood—how the *now,* relentless and horrific, throttles not only bodies but imagination, hearts. Stealing not only lives, but our sense of living, of self.

For months, my gaze had been fixed on the worst imaginable images, my mind swarmed by a daily swelling host of ghosts. I slept and dreamed of fires, woke to a world that dreamed our death anew each hour. Legacy media and elite institutions played host to a discourse in which our killing was premise, opinions ranging only on the rate and style. In New York City, I moved through my corner of empire, keffiyeh-clad and clenched, pelted with dirty looks and bracing always for a blow. Where, in all of this, had I felt *loved as a Palestinian?*

Growing up, my parents, generous, heaped me with love in both English and Arabic—*we love you, Sarah, bnhabik habibti.* In those early years, these words were less like language, something closer to flesh. *Love*—that vowel of *o* like arms outstretched, *v* a cozy velvet close. The throaty heave of ح, the heft of حب pressing, bearing me. I would not have guessed, then, that this affection might have borders, rules. As for *Palestinian*—I loved my little *tatreez thobe*, my Sittoo's ورق عنب and مسلسلات. I loved the small silver necklace my father brought back to Illinois after his long trip, but I did not understand that its finger-shaped pendant was a country, bought in a place called Quds, Jerusalem. Still, I wore it proudly, the little appendage pointing directly at my heart.

In those days, my body was a homeland, unquestioned and at peace. It was neither *Palestinian* nor *American,* but soft, sturdy, and mine. I had my father's athletic limbs and sturdy torso, a frame that would have once been built for farming; our *fellahi* family grew barley and wheat. Knowing none of this, I simply loved the way it carried me from delight to delight—oceans and baseball diamonds, swing sets and zoos. Exuberant, scabbed, and sensitive, I felt nothing but friendship toward my appetites—the rhythms of hunger and satisfaction, the invitation of curiosity toward the delicious and the new. Flesh and urges, an easy partnership. The world, a feast.

Eventually I did begin to know our name: *Palestinian*. At first it meant belonging, a source of abstract but profound pride. I did not hear the word *diaspora,* but did know us as disparate, a far-flung family. How my father loved to recount the ways our relatives, all refugees, distinguished themselves from the UAE to Canada—*doctors! engineers!* We wandered the world like a blessing, trading on our good behavior, our immaculate work. *Your cousin is an award-winning optometrist in England! Mashallah, Amu Mohammed's sons are all doctors, pharmacists, and architects!*

Only occasionally did my father speak outright the coded warning of this praise. *Some of them think we're bad people,* my father sometimes admitted, his voice dropping, dulled. Even as a child, I knew which *them* he meant. It was their world we moved in. Theirs, the right to arbitrate. Ours, the burden of proof. *Some of them think we're bad people, but when they meet us they see how hardworking and decent we are,* he continued. *We can change their minds.*

These were our frontiers.

And so I learned *Palestinian* as dual: in privacy, it made us lush, loud. Delicious and *kareem*. But outdoors, *Palestinian* receded behind American accents and manners. *Palestinian,* not a secret, but almost. Revealed only slowly, almost apologetically, cashing in on earned goodwill. Hoping this conversation to pass quickly. Hoping, mostly, to pass.

It was not love we looked for.

As a teenager, I began to notice Palestine as a wounded body on TV. Mostly, my father turned these news segments down, or off. He grew quiet, too, his face darkening, opaque. On my own, I snuck in research about our history, filling in the vague outline of the Nakba, our Catastrophe. But there was something furtive to my internet searches, my trips to the library. Somehow, my curiosity felt illicit. Even as *Palestinian* was an exhortation to excellence, *Palestine* lived among us as a ghost. Faint, weightless, a silence thinly fringed by words. Its geography, apparational. It hologrammed between the blue covers of our passports, disappeared each time we opened them.

Palestine, the impossible horizon, the absence that explained our presence in one city, then the next. *Gaza* was unreachable, spoken only in a handful of gauzed stories, her form inscrutable.

For a long time, I did not think to press this silence. It made sense to shroud our tragedy this way—the hush that gathers around the names of the dead.

Of course, Palestine itself was never dead, but with time I would learn the chronology of our graves: 'Ibdis, our ancestral home just east of Gaza, razed in 1948. Deir al-Balah, Gaza: first a refuge, then beloved home, my father's birthplace by the sea. *Nakba,* followed by *Naksa:* 1967, loss multiplied by loss. From there, rippling displacements, a series of false starts. My father and his family displaced from Gaza to Jerash, Jeddah, Cairo, Baghdad, then Jeddah again. Though he found kinship among many of his Arab neighbors, others flung xenophobic taunts. In turn, the Arab governments betrayed them too, treating refugees like pawns while their lips sang of Quds.

In this way, *Palestinian* too often meant *unwanted,* injustice recapitulated in his mother tongue. Over and over, *Palestinian* cost him—his student visa, his seat in medical school, job opportunities. Again and again, the reminder: how far he was from home.

Only my father knows when his goodbyes began. What indignity turned him that first degree, shifting his horizons west. Reluctant at first, then hopeful, he listened to the stories told by *cultural ambassadors* from the US: how their country offered equal opportunity, the chance for all to thrive. He cast his lot for a student visa and, at twenty-three, crossed the Atlantic for the first time. He boarded the plane buoyant and hungry, ignoring the gnaw of fear.

غ ر ب – *Strange, West, alien.* غربة , *ghourba.* Untranslatable, a word used to describe the place-state of being separated from one's people, home—and in some way, from oneself. Something like exile, but also existential—one is *in* ghourba, suffers *from* ghourba, becoming self-estranged, *ghareeb*. Body as uncanny, contaminated by West-ness. Body as boat in a sea of strangers, cargoed with empty space. Notoriously untreatable, it is rarely fatal. Often, it is the cost incurred to survive.

Nakba: the great separation. *Ghourba*: the intimacy of this loss.

My father's *ghourba* accumulated quietly, beneath the thrum of the new. It arrived in the exhaustion of English, the bite of snow that met him that first Sunday at O'Hare. The beep and brightness of supermarkets, the obscene boast of their stocked shelves. The sodium—benzoate, glutamate—coating his tongue with synthetic pleasure, leaving his bowels to ache. The bitter tears of his mother on every call back home. His nationality was listed as *Egyptian* because according to the university registrar, *Palestine* was not a place.

For years I did not recognize that ghostly vein, pulsing haunt beneath his skin. So much never told to me—how, left of both his seas, he had traded pieces of himself. Bought strangerhood, found consolation. Employment, immigration papers, a wife. A narrative arc, sweet and cresting. Me, firstborn, birthed beyond the reaches of his disaster. A beginning, an end to our fugitivity.

But it was not only his *ghourba* he tried to silence with his will—he also hoped to preempt mine. In the delivery room, he beheld me: leggy, cowlicked, and divine. His heart, trembling with the aggression of love that arrived. Determining: he would make his life a protective rift. Moat me with his silence, keeping history at bay. His exile, alchemized into my belonging: a home unthreatened by invasion, poverty, or bomb. In his affection, he swore to protect me even from the mention of these griefs. Perhaps, in this way, he sought not only to ensure my peace, but find his own through me. Wanting to believe that together we had become—*Palestinian, but American. Accepted. Beloved.*

And I believed him. Or perhaps I knew he needed me to be this: an embodied affirmation that this second-choice life was, after all, a prize. Growing, he gave me his childhood as contrast. My shoes were Velcro, festooned with jelly flowers. He went barefoot until age six. The faucets in my house were generous, their liquid clear and sweet. As a boy in Gaza, my father drank from containers that quivered with colonies of bugs. His first soccer ball was homemade; I had more than one. These, the small ways he coached me in our immigrants' script. Never naming the large horrors, fixing instead on America's truest currency: comfort. Convenience, the consolation produced by the same system that created our exile.

Like love, *ghourba* was a presence I needed no words to prove. I sensed my responsibility to carry, enact my father's dream. I was like him: I wanted to protect. So I made my Baba's smile a language, and with it I spelled myself. Giving him what I could: a blossoming daughter. *Palestinian* as he taught me to be: hard-working, willing, good. For a time, it felt easy. For a time, it felt true.

How much did our childhoods echo one another, beneath the stories of difference?

Often, my father betrayed himself, slipped into a reminiscing, which resurrected a father I had never seen. A boyish light in his eyes, his smile summoning an extra dimple as he called back Falasteen. This was not the generic nostalgia that framed the stories of a distant Nakba, the proxy pathos of Fairuz's croon. This حنان was *his*—love and its missing, as particular as skin. Gaza, here, was jeweled waves, the taste of pigeons, my father standing in his first-grade class, showing off his reading skills. The mischief of his brothers, the purr of their cat Hamdan. A night sky with no war. Retelling, my father's frame grew tender, lifting with a kind of music, flickering both young and large. A truth I would later learn to discern—that our bodies do not lie. His still knew the ground that made him. The place he most felt alive.

It is here that *ghourba* cuts deepest. Not in the sorrow of strangeness, but in the specter of forgone joy. Better not to name it—all that yearning. The world our flesh carries, names. The world it longs to know.

My first few crushes passed through me, unacknowledged. I was unprepared to recognize queerness—it was outside the realm of what I knew as possible. By then, as a preteen, I was growing practiced at policing myself. My developing body, its prickling urges, had just begun to reveal itself as a source of shame. My parents were alarmed by my sudden curves, instructing me to keep my clothes relatively long and loose. *It's for your own good. Trust us. You don't want boys looking at you.* They considered themselves moderate. We lived in Saudi Arabia then, where my father rolled his eyes at the morality police, bemoaning the obligatory abayas, which baked me, my mother, and sisters in the heat. *These people are extremists,* he explained, but after I hit twelve, he did not want me wearing shorts above the knee.

And so I knew my body as a site for male contestation, a territory endangered yet threatening. I was learning to judge femme bodies according to cruel hetero-male codes—learning, too, to feel inferior. At the same time, pressured by my parents, I was slowly giving up my friendships with boys. Before, I had taken pride in their hard-earned acceptance, won by proving myself the scrappiest member of our baseball team. In their stead, I began befriending girls.

At first, I had found these connections both intimidating and unexciting—most of the girls I knew were disinterested in the sports I deeply loved. Yet I was not only a tomboy—I was bookish, too. In drama classes, girl scouts, and reading groups, I found a tribe like me. Our intimacies, innocent and complex—we dressed for each other, cooed over each other, spent Friday nights in shared bunkbeds or stretched on each other's floors.

In theory, these spaces were unfettered, absent the rules of propriety and modesty my parents insisted on for coed groups. Yet somehow, I felt more tension in these rooms—a little giddy, a little shy. The boys I knew were straightforward, if thrilling—all their tussling and teasing, the constant, crude negotiations of rank. But these girl-creatures were exquisite, and various. Tender and volatile. I felt an overt longing for their approval, but I thought nothing of the way my eyes followed their bodies. My desire to touch their cheeks, their hair.

My first kiss was nonconsensual. A friend's older brother, a white boy, his arm pulling all of me to him. His mouth and hands, a shock. *How did he know he could do that?*

This boy never meant much to me, but I learned I liked being touched. I listened to this sudden appetite. I let him touch and touch me again. In stolen corners, my body moved as if touching was what it was made to do.

When my parents discovered us, I learned how much my body could destroy. My father's dark face paling, lips spittled, eyes wide. Until now, neither of us had dreamed that I might break the rules. Worst of all, perhaps—I had violated *our culture.* This, he told me, was not our way. I had strayed *as a Palestinian girl.*

I had not known a pain like this. I had been, on a few occasions, blistered by my father's temper. My peace-seeking heart recoiled at his anger, but I discovered his disappointment stung far worse. A glimpse of his sorrow was all it took to liquify my young rebellion into guilt. How little he had ever asked of me—only to play my role in the story of our family's honor and happiness. It was a beautiful story. It was the least that I could do.

The boy who pawed me was American, a missionary's son.

When, after shaking loose from this boy, I developed a crush on his sister, *irony* was a concept I was still too young to grasp. I was, however, certain that my attraction was absurd.

We were in the pool, playful whacking each other with foam noodles, the water around us spraying like cold fireworks. We paused, and I watched dusk light glide in rivulets down her face and neck. A drop gemmed the tip of her slim nose; an impulse to kiss her flared from my solar plexus to my throat. For an instant, this kiss existed, a throb of possibility. A moment later, my mind surged to respond: *Girls can't kiss girls!* The thought arrived not as a moral judgement, but with the cool swiftness of truth. There was an order, there were borders, to the world. In its midst, my body could be a faulty compass, its inclinations incorrect. Unnatural.

In this, I sensed danger. It was not simply that my erotic inklings had led so recently to parental rage. There was something about *this* desire, a strangeness I could only interpret as deviant. My instincts told me that such a feeling, if admitted, threatened my belonging. That to yearn wrongly was to identify with a realm other than the one assigned to me. It was to be alien, the transgression in my flesh rendering me an exile from within.

And so I moved urgently to silence, stifle, this appetite. As my friend swam toward me, I ditched my noodle and dove away.

These moments compounded. Most of the decisions were internal, a honed art of freezing the first sparks of desire. For years, I did not count this as a cost—in many ways, it was a comfort. So much simpler to close off not just from lust, but all the ways my body tried to speak. I was a happy child, yes—but this happiness was brittle, stretched taut over an internal restlessness. Inexplicable and visceral, this grumbling began in earnest after I spent five years in Jeddah from ages eight to thirteen. There, I tasted, if not total belonging, a new wholeness between my interior and outward-facing worlds. Moving *back* to the United States afterward, I was told I was *returning home.* It was at this age I began to deny myself food—as if I might starve into submission the part of me that trembled, that potent and opaque sense I was not where I belonged.

Return, عودة—if there is an antidote to *ghourba*, it is this. And it would be unfair to say my family had surrendered this hope. For years, this dream rode the movements of resistance. The call of the *fedayeen*, the promises of the PLO. Some, like my father, felt it rekindling in the promise of Oslo. But bodies, aging in *ghourba*, became compendiums of possibilities desecrated and denied. Imaginations may succumb to repetition, and it must have seemed that the falsehoods, the losses, would never end. With time, it came to seem that the colonizer's dream was where we had always lived. The emergency had become The World As It Is.

I visited Palestine first at seventeen. My father took me and my three siblings, and for ten days we brushed against what might have been. Here, again, I saw that specter of my father at home, at ease. How his body glided down Quds's crooked streets, how proudly he perched in taxis, how voraciously he befriended everyone. The adopted idioms of the Saudi dialect melted from his speech, ringing out in a full-throated Falastini *felahyi* accent. We followed behind him, our joy at first filtered through our fathers', then becoming our own. Our bodies moving, eating, creating and receiving memories.

Of course, we saw the danger—the violence of occupation, the Nakba sprawling and intimate. Of course, we knew our ten-day tour only skimmed the reality of what it would mean to stay. Yet for moments, we lost sight of our imminent departure. How unnatural it seemed, then, to separate from this place. When the time came to board our flight back to the US, we took our seats quietly. Blinking, almost groggy. As if emerging from a dream, or sliding into one.

I was set to start at a prestigious university that year. My father was delighted, so relieved as I walked toward success, security. *Palestinians are so smart!* he affirmed, *You'll show them all.* A reminder: this was our arena—to be the best among the strangers, making our distant homeland proud.

I came close to kissing a woman only once. She made the move, at a party, our bodies sheathed in music, dark. Before I had time to react, I had already pulled away.

The next morning, sitting at a cluttered table in my shared college suite, I probed my memory of the night before. Bleary, my guard a little lax, I replayed the thrill of that almost-kiss. For a moment, it was not frightening, only a relief to release the vise grip of denial. With this, an imaginative space opened, swarmed with impossibilities. Briefly, I contemplated a life in which I became, like many of my peers, open about my desire. In this world, I would, at last, let my body speak. And perhaps, at last, I would know sex as some claimed to—not as a meager site of anxiety but an appetite, a feast.

But even as fantasy, these scenarios appeared flat and hollow. I could not, really, access this dream. Unpracticed, my imagination faltered, rendering only dim, generic projections of what my queer life might be. Between me and these abstract longings sat the solid fact of my father, and of my love for him. I could not bear the thought of my happiness pitted against his. I feared, too, admitting how much protecting him had already cost me—a partial banishment, an estrangement from my body entrenched by many years.

And yet, I chose it again—this inward *ghourba*. Better, I decided, than outward exile.

And so, it went. Tolerably. For a time.

Except for this: my body fought the lie. Inside me, they swelled: the mutiny, the contradictions I had tried to starve. Drumming in me—*not this, not this, not this,* a doubt, a panic beneath my living, contradicting my outer happiness and accomplishments. *Not this,* said the flesh, *not this,* though English never was its tongue. It curled itself against my clenched teeth, tongue bent, biting its — لا

I can't say my father was happy when I began taking solo trips to Palestine. I returned for the first time as a college freshman, venturing across the border from my summer studies in Amman. The journey was an ordeal—hours of interrogation, a confusion of taxis, a hostel that smelled like rotting fruit. But when I woke that first morning, I felt something new. Despite the discomfort of my surroundings, my body held a sort of hush, as if some great, lifelong commotion had dropped away. Or perhaps it was simply the absence of an ache, the symmetry of spirit and geography—relief.

Later, calling my father from the Damascus Gate, I heard the tension in his voice. But he softened as my days ticked by without major incident. Our WhatsApp chat streamed with my photos—of steaming *ka'ak* and silver olive groves, of soft flocks and his beloved sea—and his delighted replies. *That's so Palestinian!* he replied when I described my adopted family in Nablus, how, for a summer, they made me their own. *So Palestinian,* he said, as I told him of my students, children, flying kites in the face of armed settlers. *That's Palestine.*

Over the years I made many, if often difficult, trips to the land. Each time, he shared a little deeper in my determined joy. Beginning slowly to see a world that could hold both his daughter and Falasteen.

When I finally did kiss a woman, it was me who made the move. This touch, too, spread a hush of recognition, relief, through my limbs. Something new that was more like remembering.

Coming out was not the gesture that called to me. Mine was a gradual shift, less of an arrival than a decision to embark. It came over time, as I recovered from my eventually life-threatening anorexia. As I healed, my body gathered power, and with it, a kind of speech. The flesh has a way of telling truths the mind tries to resist. In my case, this fight had left scars, a trail of years I'd lived, and loved, only partially. I did not yet know what it would cost me to move in conversation with desire. And I had grown tired of this—absence as a mode, denial as a home. There had to be some other way.

Yet my equivocations, all those years ago in my dorm, were not unfounded. As I knew, and then experienced, it is no simple thing to seek a queer life in a world built on enforced conformity. Trying to find my way, I found brittle, depoliticized bubbles labeled LGBT. Within, a certain set of bodies and activities were sanctioned, so long as they adhered to the unspoken expectation of respectability. This, I was told, was called protection, or even *pride*. Yet here, I found little love for my body *as a Palestinian*. The fact of my flesh was a challenge, a threat. *Liberation* for me and my kin would mean more than parades. *As a Palestinian,* I am an embodied demand for decolonization. A call to divest from the homo-nationalist machine.

My community, then, would be not received but built. Loved into existence, one connection at a time—at queer raves and on beaches, yes, but also in organizing spaces, vigils, and protests. Within this extended family, I am held and sometimes humbled. Challenged and touched. At its best, it is a place where the air might thrum with a sense of erotic yearning that extends far beyond sex. A sense of an elsewhere, another world we need and might create. Just as a free Palestine would upend the current order, so would a liberated queerness require monumental change. In the words of queer scholar and theorist José Esteban

Muñoz, *We are not yet queer, but we can feel it as the warm illumination of a horizon imbued with potentiality ... The future is queerness's domain.* We are not yet queer, but our *ghourbas*, our inborn fealty to far horizons, point the way.

A few weeks into the escalating genocide in Gaza, I called my father, phone smoldering against my ear. Amid the reeling horror, I was trying to check in daily. I worried about him, living in a small North Carolina town, the only Palestinian he knew for miles. Normally, our phone calls were long, ambling, animated. Now, our conversations were mostly stammers, punctuated by long pauses and heavy breaths. Usually, there was news of more relatives in Gaza, dead. I tried not to overwhelm him with my grief. Instead, I asked gently, clumsy questions. *Have you eaten? Slept?* I could hear him straining to access language. *How could they ... How could this ... what about ...*

Then one day, midsentence—silence.

My mother picked up the phone. *He's just ... frozen,* she told me. And then I heard his sobs.

Put him back on the phone, Mom, please.

What I heard was the force and weight of years. *I'm so sorry, habibti. I'm so sorry you have to be Palestinian. Because of me. I'm so sorry I brought you into this.*

What makes you feel loved as a Palestinian?

That day, in front of the mostly white audience, I answered, *sacrifice.* I spoke of the need for them to take risks, to speak out against genocide, and be willing to pay the price for their solidarity, whether personally, professionally, or politically—until Palestine is free.

But what, between Palestinians, should our loving do?

If I have an answer, it must have to do with truth. To love *as a Palestinian* is to love through private and public Nakba, amidst our displacements and layered, ongoing loss. To love a Palestinian is to offer oneself as place, as permission, for grief. To love, Palestinian to Palestinian, is to search for the courage to witness one another in our yearnings, in our unscripted and unruly needs. It is to hold *ghourba* open, together, knowing this is a necessary wound. Together, daring to accept *ghourba* as a call to return. To know that to hear this is to ruin one kind of life. It is to love life enough to do this. To love one another home.

End Note

by Hannah Moushabeck

All my life, I have cut myself into pieces and found communities among the severed parts. I learned of fat liberation from my first therapist in my 20s, which was how old I was when it first occurred to me that maybe there was nothing wrong with my size. I was raised among Palestinians, making sure I knew the correct way to make lentil soup, how to identify Western propaganda, and how to appeal to American humanity when ours should not be the one in question. Queerness was where I found my people, before I was ever attracted to another human. It was where I could breathe and thrive.

In the aftermath of October 7th, like most diaspora Palestinians, I answered the call from my kin abroad and reshaped my world for the cause. I could no longer stand to be in spaces that ignored the struggle of my people. While I started to stitch parts of myself together, I shed people whom I will never miss. Palestine became my rallying call in these adjacent movements, and I witnessed the web of oppression starting to solidify in my understanding.

In commissioning this anthology—the first of its kind to be published in the United States—I initially believed its purpose was to educate a Western audience that believes pinkwashed lies.

"See! We exist!" it would say. But as our authors started writing, and as George and I spent time with each piece, I realized that I was wrong.

It is not our job to prove we exist, or as Hala Alyan says, "audition for our humanity." As I read and reflected on these powerful essays, poems, stories, and art works, I selfishly began to understand these were written for me. A younger me. A divided, fragmented, Hannah who never knew she could be whole. To see my rage, joy, righteousness and indignation reflected back at me through these pieces has prompted a healing I could never have anticipated.

This book is for us. For those who have been told you can't be both queer and Palestinian. It is for our ancestors, undeniably there, but erased by history. It is in service of our liberation, which is inevitable and on its way.

Contributor Biographies

Afeef Nessouli (he/him) is a journalist and host of "_With Afeef Nessouli." He recently spent nine weeks in Gaza as a humanitarian aid worker with Glia International and as a reporter with *The Intercept.* He is a recipient of the 2025 FIJ and Pulitzer Center grant awards. He also currently teaches Communication & Social Media at Parsons School of Design in New York City. He previously worked for Spotify and *The Wall Street Journal*'s daily news podcast, "The Journal," *The Daily Show with Trevor Noah*, CNN, and as a legal adviser to the United Nations Special Rapporteur on Torture for the Carter Center. His current reporting focuses on US politics, the Middle East, and queer stories around the world.

Al Maqdisi (he/him) is a Palestinian photographer based in Jerusalem. He regularly contributes to various print publications and online platforms. He has also participated in multiple collaborations and solo exhibitions internationally. His artistic work tackles representations of queer and political identities. Through his portraits he aims at capturing the human physique that reflects expressions of emotions and states of mind. Working with photographs, Al Maqdisi has created diverse series while using different mediums: digital photography, polaroid, and medium format film.

Bint Bandora (she/they) is the alias of a queer Palestinian artist whose work emerges from her deep love and longing for the Homeland. Born into diaspora, but always connected to her roots, she uses her mixed media artistic practice to explore themes of displacement, belonging, queerness, and grief. Using illustration, collage, comics, and fiber arts, Bint Bandora turns her own personal experience into visual stories that boldly speak to the greater, collective struggle. For Bint Bandora, her creative practice is a love letter to Palestine and a reminder that liberation is coming.

Elias Jahshan (he/him) is a Palestinian-Lebanese writer. He's the editor of the groundbreaking anthologies *This Arab Is Queer* (Saqi Books; 2022) and *This Queer Arab Family* (Saqi Books, 2025). *This Arab Is Queer* was a 2023 Lambda Literary Awards finalist and shortlisted for the 2023 Bread and Roses Award. His short memoirs have been anthologized in *Arab, Australian, Other* (Picador, 2019) and *Ask the Night for a Dream* (Palestine Writes Press, 2024). Elias is a former editor of *Star Observer*, Australia's oldest queer media outlet, and has been published in *The Guardian, Gay Times, The New Arab, My Kali,* and more.

Eman Abdelhadi (she/they) is a scholar, organizer, and writer based in Chicago. She co-wrote the revolutionary sci-fi novel *Everything for Everyone: An Oral History of the New York Commune, 2052–2072* (Common Notions Press, 2022), co-edited a "Queer Palestine" issue of *Pinko* magazine published in 2024, and edited a special issue of *Public Humanities* called "Palestine as Paradigm: How Gaza Transformed the World." She writes a regular column for *In These Times* magazine and is an Assistant Professor at the University of Chicago. Her book *Impossible Futures: Why Women Leave American Muslim Communities* is forthcoming with the University of Chicago Press.

George Abraham (he/they) is a Palestinian American poet, essayist, critic, performance artist. They are the author of *When the Arab Apocalypse Comes to America* (Haymarket, 2027) and *Birthright* (Button Poetry, 2020), which won the Arab American Book Award and was a Lambda Literary Award finalist. They are the editor at large of Mizna and coeditor of *Heaven Looks Like Us: Palestinian Poetry* (Haymarket, 2025), which was long-listed for the Palestine Book Award.

Hannah Moushabeck (she/her) is a Palestinian-American book worker who was raised in a family of publishers and booksellers. Hannah has worked in publishing for over a decade and now runs Interlink Publishing, the only Palestinian-owned publisher in the United States, alongside her family. Her debut picture book, *Homeland: My Father Dreams of Palestine* (Chronicle Books, 2023), won the New England Book Award and the Arab American Book Award.

Maria (she/her) is a Palestinian community organizer, educator, and multidisciplinary artist located in The West Bank, 48' Palestine.

Mejdulene Bernard Shomali (she/her) is a queer Palestinian poet and associate professor of Women's, Gender, and Sexuality Studies at Williams College. She is the author of *Between Banat: Queer Arab Critique and Transnational Arab Archives* and the poetry chapbook *agriculture of grief: prayers for my father's dementia.*

Micaela Kaibni Raen (she/her) is a Queer Palestinian mother, cultural worker, and femme-dyke creator. She is most known for Queer Tatreez, a style of visual poetics inspired by Indigenous Palestinian Tatreez embroidery. A Tin House Alum, she has been awarded the Yalda Award for Poetry. Her work has been featured in *Bint el Nas, Mizna, Qafiyah Review, Bombay Gin Journal, Yellow Medicine Review, The Poetry of Arab Women, El Ghourabaa, Ask the Night for a Dream,* and *Heaven Looks Like Us.*

Nadia Shammas (she/they) is a Palestinian-American writer from Brooklyn, New York, now living in Toronto, Canada. She is best known as the writer and co-creator of *Squire* (HarperCollins, 2022), a Harvey Award-winning YA Middle Eastern fantasy graphic novel co-created with Sara Alfageeh. Her other original work includes *Where Black Stars Rise* (Tor Nightfire) and *Ms. Marvel: Stretched Thin* (Scholastic).

Noor Aldayeh (they/them) is an artist, writer, and cultural worker from Los Angeles, California, currently residing in New York City. The queer child of Southwest Asian and North African (SWANA) immigrants (Syrian father and Jordanian-Palestinian mother), much of Al-Dayeh's work critiques orientalism and the orientalist gaze as it pertains to intersectional identities within the SWANA region. A graduate of Emory

University with highest honors, their senior thesis and post-graduate work documents the lives of queer SWANA women and gender-nonconforming individuals and their safe spaces. They also volunteer at the Lesbian Herstory Archives in Park Slope, Brooklyn, focusing on the preservation and archiving of queer SWANA (especially Palestinian) individuals, stories, and histories.

Noor Hindi (she/they) is a Palestinian-American poet. Her debut collection of poems, *Dear God. Dear Bones. Dear Yellow* (Haymarket Books, 2022), was an honorable mention for the Arab American Book Award. She is the coeditor of *Heaven Looks Like Us: Palestinian Poetry* (Haymarket Books, 2025).

Randa Jarrar (she/he/they) is the author of the memoir *Love Is an Ex-Country*, the novel *A Map of Home,* and the collection of stories *Him, Me, Muhammad Ali.* She is also a performer. She lives in Los Angeles.

Sara Solara (she/her) is a YA science fiction and fantasy author represented by Rebecca Podos at Neighborhood Literary. As a queer and multiracial writer (Palestinian, Colombian, white), she crafts stories born of her mixed existence, from a deep-seated rage and a burning hope for liberation. Her work has also been published in *Thyme Travellers: An Anthology of Palestinian Speculative Fiction*.

Sarona Abuaker (she/her) has been published in *Berfrois, MAP Magazine, KOHL, Ludd Gang, Senna Hoy,* and other platforms. Her debut poetry collection, *Why so few women on the street at night* is a queer phenomenology of collective Palestinian futurisms and memory building. She co-developed with Dr. Danah Abdulla *Countless Palestinian Futures*, a game that aims to stimulate the imagination by helping people develop tangible outcomes and ideas around Palestinian futures.

S. is a Palestinian American writer with roots in Gaza.

Tariq Ra'ouf (he/they) is a Palestinian-American writer and activist, whose work explores identity, personal empowerment and the impacts of capitalism and colonialism on our everyday lives. With over a decade of experience in entertainment and cultural journalism, he's learned how to turn his own experience of assimilation and whitewashing into a weapon against empire, and a tool of societal self-reflection. His work centers on cultural and political awakening, grief, and resistance.

Mx. Yaffa (they/she) is an author, organizer, and culture worker. Yaffa's poetry, non-fiction, and fiction books have been sold globally and translated to various languages. Yaffa is the author of the poetry collections: *blood orange, desecrated poppies, sage,* and *thistle,* the non-fiction essay collections: *whispers beneath the orange grove, living to 99, letters from a living utopia,* and *be better broken*, and the editor of the anthology: *Inara*. Yaffa is also the Executive Director of the Muslim Alliance for Sexual and Gender Diversity. Yaffa's service to liberation spans continents. They dream of living in a liberated Falasteen soon.